Clocks Locks and Danger

White Tree Publishing

Clocks Locks and Danger

A Button Up Detective Agency Cozy Mystery #1

by

Lizzie Lewis ©2021

This Paperback ISBN: 978-1-912529-85-8

Also available as an eBook ISBN: 978-1-912529-86-5

Full list of books and updates on
www.whitetreepublishing.com

Published by
White Tree Publishing
Bristol
UNITED KINGDOM

Chapters

Chapter 1

My name is Janika Jones. I'm sitting in my car looking at a coffee shop called Button Up. It wasn't called Button Up when I was at school, but that's not important. What is important is whether I'm about to make the stupidest mistake of my life. The office and living apartment above the café sounded ideal when I read the advertisement. A minimum one-year tenancy. If I take it, there can be no going back. I'll be stuck here in Craidlea for twelve whole months. Is this really what I want?

It's strange how memories come flooding back, taking you by surprise. I remember a girl at school called Button. Abi Button, or the Happy Button as she was known by her friends. I can picture her now – blonde, popular, pretty and always laughing. I've not been back to this town since I was fifteen, which is when I went to live in Poland with my English mother and Polish father. And that certainly was a culture shock – for my mother as well as for me.

I'm wondering what has brought me back to Craidlea after what must be ... yes, eighteen years. I don't have the happiest memories of school in England, although I think I'm mostly to blame for that. I was too quiet. I can see myself now, a rather withdrawn girl who tended to get picked on.

I smile to myself. That has certainly changed since Sam died. The coroner was all primed up to announce a verdict of suicide – before I stuck my oar in. Suicide? I knew differently. Sam, that's my husband, might have been weighed down by our money problems, but he was never going to take his own life. Take his life for what? Our life insurance? Our policy had lapsed a few months earlier. We simply couldn't pay the premiums, along with other necessities.

Shortly before his death, Sam insisted that we found the money somehow to take out a new policy, because he didn't want to leave me penniless if anything happened to him. Was that some sort of premonition? Anyway, we started paying again, but the new policy stipulated that it wouldn't pay out for suicide within the first twenty-four months. We didn't see that as a problem at the time. Why would we?

Sam Jones was a detective with the CID in the huge town of Brevelstone where we first met, and where we got married just over three years ago. And now, after his sudden death, Brevelstone holds too many disturbing memories to stay there any longer. I'm not sure about the wisdom of coming back here, either. Lots of memories of school, and of my parents arguing constantly – my father not wanting to settle in England, and my mother and me not wanting to settle in Poland. It was all a bit of a mess, and unfortunately my father came out the winner.

Those school memories are troubling me now. If I hadn't been such a mouse I would have stood up for myself. Coming back to England and leaving my parents and

Bruno behind in Poland was the first properly brave thing I did in my life. The second properly brave thing was taking on the coroner and the police to get my husband's death declared a murder. And I suppose the *best* thing was doing my own detective work to help bring in a verdict of murder by person or persons unknown.

And that brings me back to where I am now, outside Button Up coffee shop. I suppose this counts as another brave move, although if I get out of my car and accept the tenancy on the apartment above the café, that will surely be the *most* heroic thing I've ever done. I mean, what woman decides to open a private detective agency on her own? But I think Sam would be proud of me, following in his footsteps, but following in his footsteps privately, not with the police.

I go to open the door of my old car and tell the proprietor, Abi Wells, that I've come for the four o'clock appointment to view the apartment. But I can't pull the handle. It's like I'm paralysed. Do I really want to go ahead with this? I smile to myself, and say loudly, "Come on, Janika, see it through, girl. You don't have to say yes, even if it's the most charming living accommodation and office you've ever seen. And it won't be, anyway."

I look up at the two windows above the coffee shop. One of them has an old blind hanging crookedly, and the other has a sign saying, "Jennings Accountancy Services."

To my tidy mind, I realise there's an apostrophe missing at the end of Jennings, but that doesn't matter. I'm not exactly going to tell him. Anyway, I gather Mr Jennings retired a few weeks ago. The handle of the car door isn't really jammed. So why am I sitting here hesitating?

I check the rear view mirror and get briskly out of the car. As I approach Button Up I catch sight of myself in the large café window. Inside, I can see tables and chairs, and three or four customers. Reflected in the glass I see myself. There is nothing remarkable about my appearance. I'm nearly five foot four, with short mousy brown hair and the sort of face and figure that doesn't attract attention. If I want to be critical about myself, the kindest thing I can say is that I fall into the gap between being good-looking and being downright plain.

In fact, I'm average altogether in my looks, which is probably perfect if you want to be a private investigator. Unlike the glamorous actresses who play private investigators in daytime television programmes, nobody notices you if you're average looking. With several outfits, two or three wigs and different glasses, and several shades of makeup, I'll just blend in. Anyway, that's what I'm hoping.

I open the café door and a young man wearing a black and cream striped jacket smiles and offers to show me to a table. I explain I've come to meet Mrs Wells. To my amazement, it's not Mrs Wells who comes from behind the service counter, smiling.

It's Abi Button. I've not seen her for eighteen years, but I'd recognise her anywhere. And she's certainly not lost her looks. She's managed to stay slim, apart from round the hips. These memories give me quite a jolt.

"I've got an appointment with Mrs Wells," I say. "It's

to view the apartment and office."

Abi Button says she *is* Mrs Wells, and she seems to recognise me too, because she calls me Janika Bartol. Then we look at each other and laugh. I've already noticed the wedding ring, so the Wells bit makes sense.

"I didn't realise it would be you," Mrs Wells says. "I didn't connect the name. And please call me Abi. I'm sure you remember me as Abi Button. When I got married, we didn't want to change the name of the coffee shop."

I'm wondering where the Up bit comes from, and no doubt I'll learn that later – if I decide to stay. I point to the ceiling, hoping we're not going to stand here reminiscing about school, cooking up bad memories. "If I could just have a look, please. It sounds ideal."

Abi looks closely at me for a moment and smiles. "We must have been about fifteen years old last time we saw each other, and we both *still* look so young."

Do we? I need to agree with Abi and I return the smile. "Well, we *are* young."

Abi winks at me. "Correct answer. I'm glad you said that."

She introduces me to the young man who I think has just rolled his eyes, but I can't be sure. He's called Pete Wilders. He's a student doing an evening course at the local college. He frowns slightly, and I guess he's going to ask Abi how we know each other. But hopefully when I've gone.

Abi gets a key from behind the counter and ushers me out through the door. "I'm all ready for you."

On the right hand side of the café entrance there's a

white front door set back enough from the pavement to give shelter to anyone waiting to enter. In a city centre, this place would probably be used by men who had been drinking too much at night, but there's no smell of urine here, which is certainly good news.

I can see a small intercom system, but Abi puts the key in the lock and opens the door to reveal a shabby staircase. This doesn't look promising. However, I've got more than enough money to start the detective agency, and I can manage some decorating if Abi isn't planning to sort it. I think it's important for customers, clients, call them what you will, to get a good first impression. And I certainly haven't got one yet.

Abi is leading the way up the steep wooden stairs, and she pauses for a moment. "We've not had time to clear the place after Mr Jennings retired," she explains apologetically. "So don't judge it by what you see now. We'll be decorating throughout, including the stairs. We honestly didn't expect anyone to respond to our advertisement so quickly."

At the top of the staircase a substantial door opens into a large office at the front of the building. It's as large as the coffee shop downstairs. I gasp in surprise. This office is going to be perfect. Clearly the walls have the same footprint as the coffee shop, which means the living accommodation is going to be small.

"We've been rather busy," Abi says. "Rest assured, it will be properly furnished with brand-new office equipment when you take it. ... If you take it," she adds.

Abi Button, Abi Wells, has clearly mistaken my gasp

for one of horror. The only horror would be if this old but impressive office furniture got replaced with something modern. I can picture myself sitting behind the desk, wearing a tight black skirt and matching jacket with a white blouse, looking extremely professional. Then when I go out on surveillance, I can wear one of my many different casual outfits and wigs, and no one will recognise me.

"But I love it," I protest. "It's *absolutely* my ideal office. I'm sure my clients, assuming I get any, will be set at ease by the comforting look. I mean, look at those two small leather armchairs by the window. And the antique mahogany desk and matching filing cabinet. Well, nearly matching. And the impressive office chair behind it. It even swivels. It's wonderful, Abi. A lovely dream come true."

Then I have another thought. "I take it there's wi-fi here." I mean it as a sort of joke, and Abi catches on immediately.

"Sorry, only morse code and semaphore," she says, laughing. "Seriously, there's high speed fibre-optic. Mr Jennings insisted on it. He was elderly, but he understood technology."

There's a long pause. I think Abi is wondering what to make of me. Eventually she smiles, and says, "Let me show you the living accommodation. I know you're going to want some changes there. Mr Jennings was almost as old as the furniture. When my co-owner of Button Up and I bought the business, this apartment was already furnished, complete with Mr Jennings as a sitting tenant.

He was happy with everything, so there was no point in buying new furniture."

Abi opens a dark brown wooden door leading directly into a small sitting room. I can see immediately why she has reservations about the furniture. Actually, it's not just a sitting room. It's what's called a bedsit. There's an old bed frame in the corner. Just the frame, no mattress or bedding.

"We got rid of the mattress," Abi says. "Mr Jennings had been using it for many years." She laughs, but looks embarrassed. "Old men and mattresses aren't exactly one of my favourite things."

I suspect there's more to it than that, but I certainly don't want any details. "Flatpack will be fine," I say. "And I prefer a firm mattress to a soft one. Other than that, the place is exactly what I'm looking for."

Mrs Wells seems surprised. No, I must get into the habit of calling her Abi, even though she's no longer Abi Button. Mrs Wells sounds much too formal for an old school ... not exactly friend. There must be a word for someone you were at school with but not especially friends with, but I can't think of it at the moment.

"You sound as though you're going to take it," Abi says.

It's my turn to look surprised. "Of course I am. It's perfect. I assume there's no objection to me putting my own business sign in the window. No planning restrictions or anything?"

I can see the cogs turning in Abi's head. This is a young woman with a sharp mind, mixed up with a dry sense of humour of the ridiculous. Since the private investigators' course, I've become very aware of people's expressions and body language. She's about to ask me what the business will be.

Chapter 2

I'm wrong. Instead of asking me about my business, Abi asks me if there will be two of us. She must have seen my wedding ring. I've no intention of taking it off. I'm proud of Sam and what he did for the police force in Brevelstone. I can see Abi is an inquisitive person, but I'm sure it's with the best of intentions. So I won't go as far as to call it nosiness. Not yet, at any rate.

"Just me," I explain, without actually giving any explanation. "You remembered I was Janika Bartol. Everybody, including you, deliberately pronounced Janika with a J, although it should really have been pronounced Yanika. I'm not pointing the finger at you in particular, Abi, but I think it was done to annoy me. When we went to Poland, everybody knew how to pronounce the name. But when I came back to England, I gave up. So I guess you all got it right at school. Yes, please call me Janika."

I can see the cogs still turning in Abi's head. I decide it *is* some form of nosiness, but probably nosiness in the best possible taste. "And now you're a Jones," she says.

She doesn't need to say anything more. It's time to explain how my name became Jones. We go back into the old-fashioned but professional looking office, and sit next to each other in the small leather armchairs by the window.

Abi jumps up and tries to raise the crooked blind to

let more light in, but it crashes to the ground. She shrugs, and sits down again.

Opposite, I can see living accommodation above a shoe shop. No, it's not living accommodation. It's their stockroom. I wonder how many people actually *live* in this street.

Abi clearly wants to know why I'm wearing a wedding ring. I'll have to tell her that my husband is dead. What took months flies through my mind in seconds. But I can't explain it in seconds. I wonder how to condense it, because Abi is probably needed down below in the coffee shop. But I would like to share something of my background while we're sitting here.

<><><><>

My mind takes me back almost exactly six months. The doorbell rings. I've been expecting Sam home from work. He's a Detective Constable with Brevelstone CID. I know he's been working this evening, but he's later than I expected. He has his own key, so who's ringing the bell at eleven o'clock?

We have an outside light in the porch of the small modern house we're renting, and a spy lens fitted in the door. I can see a man and a woman there, so it looks as though I'll be safe if I open the door.

"Mrs Jones?" the man says. It's a man I barely recognise from Sam's work, but behind him is a female police officer whom I do know, but not well. Detective Constable Courtney Jacobs. And they both look ... glum. There's no other word to describe them.

"I'm Detective Inspector Dickinson," the man says, as

I open the front door wider. He's probably in his early fifties, and he's almost bald. His moustache is rather straggly, too. "I know it's late, but please may we come in."

It's not really a question.

"I'm afraid we have something to tell you," Courtney says. "We'd like you to sit down."

I know police have to do this sort of thing when they bring bad news. Ask the person to sit down and then break it to them gently. Someone has died.

Are they here with news about my parents in Poland? Surely Aunt Magdalena would have let me know. She wouldn't have left it to the local police.

I don't need to be told who it is.

"It's Sam, isn't it?" I say, as Courtney gently takes hold of my arm and leads me into the sitting room.

She waits until I sit down heavily in the armchair by the fireplace. It's not really a fireplace. It's an electric fire with a surround to make it look a bit old-fashioned. I wonder why I'm even thinking about it.

"Was it an accident?" I ask, for there is no doubt in my mind that Sam is dead.

The two officers look at each other, and I'm wondering why they hesitate.

Courtney reaches across from where she's sitting on the sofa and holds my hand. I don't pull it away. There's something about Courtney that I empathise with. She's not exactly a friend, but we've met a few times socially.

"Please tell me what's happened," I say. "He's dead, isn't he?"

Courtney just nods.

"Was it an accident?" I repeat. There's something odd about the way the two police detectives keep looking at each other.

"Was he killed on a drugs raid?" I'm fishing for answers, but I know Sam is involved in an investigation into one of the large drug dealing gangs. He's been quite excited lately, telling me he's really onto something, but he says it's a bit soon to share it at work. He just needs to carry out a few more checks.

"I'm sorry," Courtney says, "but we can't say yet. There's going to be an investigation, of course."

"Where is he now? Where did he die? Was anyone else involved?" The questions keep coming before I can stop myself. "*Where* did he die?" I decide that's the most important question for now, so I repeat it.

"It was at the bridge over the Brevel by the Old Mill Factory Outlet," Detective Inspector Dickinson says. I can see drops of sweat on his moustache. This isn't easy for any of us. I need to put on a show of bravery, no matter what I'm feeling inside.

The River Brevel is quite wide by the Old Mill, and there's a high stone bridge that would probably have been quite busy when the cotton mill was active until the early 1950s. The massive building is still there, and it's recently been restored and divided up into various retail outlets, with a small museum containing several of the weaving mills that people can walk around and even touch.

This whole part of the country was an area once rich

in cotton mills. The majority of them have been demolished, and others turned into offices and workshops. Or shopping centres – like ours here in Brevelstone. I really do need to concentrate.

"*Under* the bridge?" I ask, thinking of the dark spaces underneath the arch that would be ideal for drug dealing at night. "Was he alone?"

I see Officers Dickinson and Courtney Jacobs look at each other again. It's not any sort of personal attraction. They are clearly embarrassed.

"He was on his own," DI Dickinson says abruptly. "It seems that he ... fell. I regret to say that your husband was found dead under the bridge by the uniformed police, following a phone call from a concerned member of the public."

Courtney Jacobs says, "It seems he died instantly from the fall. I'm so sorry." And she squeezes my hand harder.

I'm trying to take this in. Sam is dead. My husband will never come through the front door again with his cheery voice. I'm a widow. Should I be feeling proud that Sam died in the course of duty? I can't get my head round it. Nothing seems real. I know it's a cliché, but any moment I'm going to wake up and laugh about a bad dream. Isn't that what everybody thinks when they get news like this?

"When you say he fell, you mean as he was fighting with someone?"

"All I'm permitted to say at the moment, Mrs Jones, is that he ... fell," DI Dickinson mumbles. The man is sweating.

"On his own?" What's he saying?

Courtney Jacobs lets go of my hand and pats it gently. "We are not in a position to say what happened, Janika. Not just yet. We'll be able to reveal more details later."

"Mrs Jones," DI Dickinson says, "I'm afraid we have a small amount of business to attend to now we're here. We're going to need your computer and both your phones. Just for now. There may be information of interest to us on them."

"We only have one laptop between us," I hear myself saying, as though in a dream. "And why do you need my phone? Sam never used it."

"I'm sorry, Janika," Courtney says. "You'll get them back in a couple of days. It's just routine."

"You're welcome to our laptop, as long as you don't mess it up. But Sam had his phone with him. Presumably you can recover it."

Detective Inspector Dickinson and Detective Constable Courtney Jacobs look at each other again. Then DI Dickinson says, "No, he definitely didn't have his phone. Would you mind looking for it, in case he left it here."

I shake my head. "He wouldn't do that. Hang on, I'll ring it just in case."

My phone is in my bag, and I speed dial Sam's number. I can hear the ringing tone on my phone, but there's silence in the house. "There you are, I told you Sam had it with him."

DI Dickinson says something to Courtney that I don't

catch as I jump up to get our laptop. DI Dickinson comes with me. I'm not sure at this stage if he's trying to be helpful, or if he wants to make sure I don't leave anything behind, like a memory stick or spare hard drive.

It's ten minutes later now, and Detective Inspector Dickinson has gone, taking everything electronic he could find. Courtney Jacobs has stayed, to make sure I settle down. Settle down? I'm never going to settle down.

I'm still wondering what's happened to Sam's phone. He took it with him, so why didn't they find it when they recovered ... his body? Well, if some opportunist thief has found it, the files on there won't be much use to them.

"Sam unlocked his phone with his fingerprint," I tell Courtney. "If you do find it, it's no use bringing it back to me. All I know is that without using the fingerprint pad it needs a numeric pin, and I've no idea what it is. So I wouldn't be able to use it anyway."

Courtney is looking at me, and I have a feeling she's suspicious of any husband who keeps his phone locked. Well, if that is what she's really thinking, she's wrong. Sam and I have no secrets. Had no secrets. I'm sure of that. A detective in the CID is entitled to have secrets on his phone. Work secrets, of course. Anyway, in the evening he would often pass me the phone and let me browse through the photographs he'd taken during the day. When the phone was unlocked I had free access to everything, and I know he wouldn't have done that if there was anything compromising on there. Love you, Sam, you know I always trusted you.

If Sam really did have information on there of interest to whoever murdered him, I can only hope they didn't unlock it with his finger after he fell. I presume a dead finger works just as well as a live one. I don't feel like discussing the matter with Courtney, and I just shrug.

She offers to stay the night, and explains its part of her duties, but I tell her I would rather be on my own. It's after midnight when she leaves. I need to phone my parents in Poland, but maybe not now. It will be the early hours of the morning there. Anyway, I don't have a phone. I can't even phone my friends.

<><><><>

It's three days later, and I've worked myself up into a terrible state. Although DI Dickinson didn't warn me, he came back the next morning with a team with a warrant to search the house. Courtney came too, looking embarrassed. She did her best to calm me down and assure me they weren't investigating Sam.

They already have Sam's fingerprints on record, and now they've taken mine. Simply to rule out our fingerprints on any equipment they find. I hope that's the reason. I don't have a police record, so I shouldn't really be anxious.

They have reason to believe Sam left a notebook or some other record of what he's been doing. It's possible he's put together some names, but not yet recorded them officially at work. I told them to get on with the search while I went for a walk to try and clear my head.

I couldn't keep away from the house for long, and when I got back I asked when they were going to return my laptop, because I needed it to email various people. I gathered it hadn't yet shown anything of interest, and I would get it back in a couple of days – unless there was a need to keep it for evidence. Evidence of what, DI Dickinson didn't elucidate, but he returned my phone, which meant I could contact my parents and one or two other people who needed to know.

That was two days ago. More details of Sam's death have been revealed. Horrible ones. There's going to be an inquest. Detective Inspector Dickinson, who seems to be in charge of the case, has already told me what the outcome of the inquest is going to be. Not *likely* to be, but what it's *going* to be. Suicide.

I can see why things are heading this way, because to someone who didn't know Sam, suicide would seem like the easy option. The landlord is about to evict us, because we're three months behind with the rent. It's not Sam's fault, and it's not really mine. We weren't even managing to keep up with the rent and utility bills when we were both working. A young detective in the local CID doesn't earn a lot. When I lost my job at the hairstylists because of the need to reduce overheads with a diminishing customer base, we ran up against a brick wall – and an uncompromising and heartless landlord.

Brevelstone is by far the largest town in the area and the economy is in a bad way, with lots of closed businesses. We were planning to move in with Sam's friends because we wouldn't be able to rent another property with such a bad financial record. Landlords always check on the status of a potential tenant. When I told my parents we were being evicted, my father told us we could stay with them in Poland, but I had some unhappy years there with Bruno Kamiński, which is the reason I came back to England four years ago. And Brevelstone is where I met my lovely Sam Jones.

Courtney has called in to check up on me, and our impending eviction somehow gets mentioned. It seems that our financial and housing status hasn't been a secret at work.

Courtney explains that Sam and I being desperately short of money won't necessarily lead the coroner to bring in a verdict of suicide. But it will be a contributing factor.

"I know Sam was working on a project to trace a major drugs distributor working out of Brevelstone. He told me he wanted to be sure of his facts before presenting the evidence to DI Dickinson."

Courtney is nodding. "That's what we were hoping to find on your laptop. So you don't know if Sam's left a notebook or folder that maybe he's hidden away for security?"

"Wouldn't it be at work?"

Courtney shrugs. "That's what we were looking for in the house search. I'm so, so sorry that your privacy was invaded like that, Janika. Especially as we found nothing of interest. Well, if you come across anything, you must let me know immediately, and I'll pass it on."

I ask Courtney about the inquest, and she tells me it's important I get a solicitor to represent me when it takes place. I ask why.

"I shouldn't be the one to be telling you this," Courtney says. "It's going to be mentioned at the inquest. A woman made a phone call."

Although I didn't really take it in at the time, I remember Detective Inspector Dickinson mentioning a phone call. I'm waiting for Courtney to go on. She doesn't seem to know exactly how to phrase it. I guess she's betraying confidences, and that annoys me. Not that she's betraying anything, but this is important information I don't know, and I clearly need to know it.

"We have a recording received from a mobile phone," Courtney explains at last, swallowing hard. "An unidentified woman phoned 999 to say she could see a man standing on the parapet of Mill Bridge, and she was afraid he was about to jump. She asked the police to come quickly."

I feel the blood draining from my face. This can't be true.

"That's all we know," Courtney says. "I'm so sorry, Janika. The woman screamed and then the phone went dead. So, that must be the moment——"

I cut her off. There's no need for Courtney to say any more. My head feels weird, but perhaps I need to know the truth. "Who is she? I want to talk to her. Perhaps there's been a mistake."

Through my tears I can see Courtney shaking her head. "We've not been able to trace her. Not yet."

"Didn't anyone get her phone number?"

"I'm so sorry, Janika. I really am. Unfortunately, the phone wasn't registered to anyone."

"Isn't that suspicious?" Is that a silly question? Actually, it's a sensible question. A very sensible question. Alarm bells are already ringing.

Courtney is shaking her head again. "Not that uncommon, Janika. A lot of people buy a phone with a SIM card with money already on it. They can go to the supermarket or a cash point to top it up. There's currently no legal requirement in England for anyone to register a phone, and since it's a lot of trouble, plenty of people don't bother. Which doesn't help the emergency services, of course."

"No way would Sam take his own life," I say, probably sounding like a robot. It's not something I've rehearsed, it's just something I know. Yes, we're short of money. Stony broke, in fact. About to lose our home, but Sam taking his life wasn't going to help. He must have known our life insurance wouldn't pay out on the new policy. And it's not likely I'll get any money from the police. Not like I would if Sam died in the course of his duties.

"Was he on duty?" I ask. "He said he was working that evening."

Courtney comes really close to me. It's like we're best friends, although we don't know each other well. It's a friendship I welcome. "He was on duty until eight," she says. "The phone call was received just after 9:30."

"Maybe Sam was following somebody and couldn't just walk away," I say. "Underneath that bridge would be a good place for drug deals to take place. He might have been hiding down there in the shadows, and afraid to leave in case they spotted him. Surely he can run up overtime if the job demands it."

Courtney shakes her head. "He definitely fell from the roadway. There's no nice way to say this, Janika, but there are traces of blood where he hit his head on one of the bridge piers on the way down. It will all come out at the inquest, so you might as well hear it from me now."

A sudden idea jumps into my head. It's obvious. "He was leaning over to see what was happening below, and he leaned over too far and fell." No, that doesn't seem right. "Apart from the woman's phone call, of course," I add.

"I'm sorry" Courtney says, patting my hand again. It's an action I find surprisingly comforting.

I'm guessing Courtney is slightly younger than me. Probably not yet thirty, but I gather she's been with the police a long time. This means she likely knows what she's talking about, but something doesn't fit easily with me. Sam isn't ... wasn't ... someone who would walk away from problems. We talked about our financial difficulties sensibly. Sam has friends in town and they've invited us to stay with them. They have a large Victorian house with plenty of room to spare. Much worse things happen to people than being temporarily homeless.

I take a deep breath, trying not to be sick. It was bad enough when Courtney came round with DI Dickinson to break the news of Sam's death. At the time I was convinced he'd been killed in the course of duty. Suicide? My whole life is falling apart.

Courtney is standing up, as though ready to leave. I pull her back onto the sofa where we've been sitting together. "What do you think, Courtney? *Did* Sam take his own life?"

I can see she doesn't want to commit herself. Or, more likely, doesn't want to tell me that she suspects he did.

"Is there *any* chance of tracking down the woman who made the phone call?" I ask. I'm probably clutching at straws, and I know I'm in denial. So would anybody be who knows Sam. Knew Sam.

Courtney Jacobs doesn't shake her head, but her expression tells me everything. "I'm sorry, Janika."

I'm not going to let it go. Yes, I'm going to need Sam's life insurance and some sort of police pension – or whatever it is for death during official duty. But that's not the point. Sam did *not* take his own life. I'd bet my *own* life on it.

I look up at Courtney and her eyes meet mine. "Courtney, you're my only hope. I don't feel like confiding in your Detective Inspector. He seems a moody sort of man."

"Roger Dickinson has things on his mind," Courtney says. "Family matters. He has a wife and two children. They've just left him."

Well, that explains why he seems rather lacking in enthusiasm. An idea occurs to me. "Courtney, will you help me investigate Sam's death?"

She shakes her head. "I'm sorry, Janika, but I'm employed by CID. I can't do unauthorised detective work."

"In that case, I'll have to do it myself."

Not that I know much about detective work. I'm wishing I'd listened more to Sam when he told me about his various exploits with catching baddies. Perhaps it's not too late to learn.

Chapter 3

Abi is looking at me closely. While I've been replaying these tragic events of six months ago in my mind, I've also been telling her just the bare bones of what happened. I can see my story has moved her to tears. This is no longer the Happy Button I remember from school.

She stands up and comes across to put her arm around my shoulders and we hug each other. There's such a large lump in my throat that I can hardly say another word.

"Janika," Abi says, "I'm just so, so sorry." She pauses for a moment. Maybe she has a lump in her own throat. "I was telling a friend how some of us at school laughed at your mother's car. The little Citroen 2CV. I said if I ever saw you again I would apologise. Please forgive me."

I can remember our Citroen 2CV, but I can't remember anyone laughing about it. Well, just a vague memory, but it certainly didn't scar me for life. It sounds as though Abi was affected more than I was.

"We took it back to Poland," I say. "My father went on by air with a lot of our luggage, and my mother and I piled the 2CV high with everything else. You should have seen it. It took four days. At the age of fifteen it was a great adventure."

Abi is smiling at me. "Do you still have it?"

I shake my head. "I think the journey to Poland brought its life to a premature end."

"Well, if you want to revive old memories, I have friends who have just restored an identical model." Abi looks at her watch. "How about I leave you alone for a few minutes? Have a good look round, sit at the desk, and imagine you're doing ... whatever work you want to do here."

"No, Abi, please stay." I know she's fishing, and I have no reason not to tell her. I can't believe she hasn't guessed anyway after hearing my story. Perhaps I need to tell her what happened next, back in Brevelstone.

<><><><>

I can't stop myself revisiting the past. Courtney is explaining that she can't jeopardise her job, but she will be able to share things that aren't confidential. She explains there's nothing to share at the moment. Her boss believes Sam took his own life, so it sounds like the coroner's work is as good as done.

What I need is a private detective. Unfortunately, we're already overdrawn at the bank, and our credit cards are maxed out. I think they're about to be cancelled, anyway. Can it be possible that Sam took his own life? I feel bad for even wondering. No, surely he wouldn't do that. *Definitely* not. We were going to stay with our friends and fight our way out of debt. I already have the offer of a possible job at a small hairdressing salon.

I tell Courtney more about our financial problems. It's going to come out at the inquest anyway, when the coroner dreams up the reason for Sam jumping from the bridge. If only I could find the woman who made the phone call.

It's going to be hard, but I need to go to the Mill Bridge and see where Sam fell. I understand from Courtney that the site has been cleaned up now. I don't even want to think what cleaning up entails. There's already been a post-mortem, but I've been advised not to see Sam's body. Apparently he fell headfirst.

Courtney says she's authorised to stay with me for the rest of the day if I like. I tell her I want to go to Mill Bridge, and she looks surprised.

"If I don't do it now, Courtney, I'll probably never go near there ever again. I need to force myself to go. I can't bear to go on my own. Will you come with me?"

We have a bit of an argument but eventually I persuade Courtney that a visit to the bridge will start to bring some sort of closure. I know it sounds crazy, but it's something I have to do.

Mill Bridge is about a mile away, and I want to walk there. I want to walk through familiar roads, trying to adjust to living in Brevelstone without Sam. But there are so many memories that I feel quite shaken when we finally arrive at the bridge.

Courtney is looking concerned. "I think you ought to leave it at this, Janika," she says, putting her arm around me again. Although I find the move reassuring, it brings out a strong emotion. I wish people wouldn't try to offer me so much physical comfort. It's more than I can bear.

I shake her free. "Which side?" I'm asking the question, almost in a trance. No, in a nightmare. But I have to see this through.

Courtney points to the left parapet. She isn't saying a word. I'm wondering if she's having as hard a time as I am. If so, I need to pull myself together and set a good example.

The parapet wall on the side of the bridge is quite low, but not low enough for anyone to fall over accidentally. The top has thick concrete slabs, probably placed there more recently to raise the height to a legal minimum. I can remember as a child wondering if I could walk across the bridge on that wall, but of course I never dared try. I certainly wouldn't want to try now.

I lean over the parapet to get a view down to the ground below. The bridge has two central arches, one on each side of the wide river.

"No!" Courtney grabs hold of my jacket and pulls me back quickly onto the walkway.

As soon as she lets go I turn to face her. I almost feel like laughing, but I don't. "I only want to look. I'm not going to jump."

Courtney nods. I think she believes me. So we haul ourselves up together and peer over the edge. Down below is a flat area of old concrete, plus some items of discarded junk. I can see where Sam must have landed. A large patch has been hosed clean, washing away all traces of my lovely husband.

I lean over a bit further, and Courtney doesn't appear bothered. It seems like she's trusting me now. Good, at least we can work as a team. I look at the stone pier on our side of the river, and can see what looks like a red stain. This must be the bloodstain she told me about. I'm not going to tell her I've seen it, because she'll probably try to prevent me from looking at it too closely. I thought she said the whole scene had been cleaned up.

I shuffle my way back onto the walkway and take a few steps further along the bridge, to be directly above the stain. Courtney comes with me, holding my arm. Perhaps she doesn't trust me so much after all. "I just want to look over here for a moment," I explain. "This must be where Sam fell from."

Once again we haul ourselves up onto the parapet and look over. Yes, it *is* blood. I'm about to point it out to Courtney. Once again she pulls me back, but not before I've seen something very small and shiny protruding from the stonework.

A couple are coming by pushing a baby in a buggy, and I don't want them to hear what I'm about to say. In fact, the bridge seems to be surprisingly popular all of a sudden. There's only a walkway on one side, and we press ourselves against the wall so the couple with the buggy can get by without actually needing to step into the road. And there's a family coming the other way from the Old Mill Shopping Outlet, carrying large bags. The fact that people have money to spend makes me sad, but not as sad as the loss of Sam.

"I need another look," I tell Courtney as soon as the walkway is clear. I'm not bothered about the cars coming and going. I just don't want pedestrians looking over, trying to see what the attraction is down below, and then asking what we're looking at. I couldn't bear to do that.

What would I say anyway? "To see where my husband died three days ago?"

It seems Courtney wants to humour me, if that's the right word. So we get onto the wall again, lying on our stomachs, leaving plenty of our bodies on the wall to save over-balancing. Could Sam really have done this, watching something suspicious going on below? I point out the blood on the stone bridge support.

"You don't want to look at that," she says. "It should have been cleaned up. I'll have a word at the station."

"Courtney," I say, "can you see something small and shiny stuck in the wall? Oh, look, look, I'm sure it's what I think it is. I can see the thin leather cord Sam kept it on."

We're finding it hard to breathe, pressed on the wall like this. "I can see something," Courtney is saying. "It's probably part of a shiny sweet wrapper that's got caught between the stones. I need to get back down. This is too uncomfortable."

We're back on the walkway now. Two middle-aged men are leaning over a little further along. I'd not realised we had company. "Just some birds," I call out to them, hoping they're not birdwatchers themselves. I don't really know one bird from another, so I don't want them to ask me what sort.

They look a bit embarrassed and walk on. That's one problem out of the way. I realise that when Sam died here, the whole area would have been deserted. The Shopping Outlet closes on the dot of eight, and by 8:30 thirty probably no one uses this road. So any cries for help at 9:30 would have gone unnoticed.

"What do *you* think you saw?" I ask Courtney. "You don't *really* think it's a sweet wrapper, do you?" Impossible though it is to believe, I'm convinced by what I've just seen. But a second opinion will be welcome.

"It looks shiny," Courtney says. "If that's what you're talking about. *Perhaps* a bit of jewellery. I could see a cord or something round it, or maybe it's a bit of a dead plant. It seems to be stuck in the stonework. What do *you* think it is?"

That's the question I've just asked her. "I think it's Sam's small gold cross," I say, but even as I say it, it sounds impossible. "But I can't see how it got stuck in the wall. If he jumped from here, or even if he was thrown over, or fell over by accident, he wouldn't have been able to stick it in the wall. So who put it there? And why? He wore it every day. I want it back."

Courtney is making a sensible suggestion. "I'm going to get in touch with the coroner's office to see if your husband was wearing his cross when he was found. If he was, then there's no need for us to do anything."

The more I think about it, the more convinced I am that we've just seen Sam's small gold cross. He was religious in a way I've never been able to understand. I went with him when he suddenly started going to church with his friends on Sundays, because I could see how much he wanted me to go, but to my shame I never even pretended to know what it was all about.

"You can do that?" I ask. "You know the coroner's number?"

Courtney has her phone in her hand. "I know a woman who does," she explains. "But we need to go somewhere quiet. This bridge is surprisingly noisy with traffic for the Shopping Outlet, and I don't want any passers-by listening in. I don't think anyone is going to interfere with what looks like a crime scene. They'd need a tall ladder. We'll only be gone a few minutes and we can keep an eye on it while I'm phoning."

I'm staring at the concrete slabs where Sam must have been just before he fell. This looks like a bloodstain. A recent one. "Come and see this, Courtney. If this *is* blood, and it's *Sam's* blood, then he didn't jump willingly. He must have already been injured."

Courtney's eyes blaze with what looks like anger. "Janika, I *definitely* need to declare this a crime scene. It seems there's been some sloppy investigation. I need to phone in."

It looks quiet below the bridge, that's for sure, but I'm not going down there. I've seen enough for one day. All I want to know is whether Sam was found wearing his cross. And I'm sure I already know the answer to that.

He was wearing it when he got dressed, but he *wasn't* found with it. I'm one hundred percent sure. Well, ninety-nine percent sure. No, one hundred percent. And if this *is* his blood on the top of the parapet, this *definitely* needs to be declared a crime scene.

On the other side of the bridge, by the Old Mill Shopping Outlet, there's a small grassy area with benches, so we cross over and make our way there.

Courtney is already dialling on her phone. She seems

to be having trouble getting someone to give her the number she needs. Presumably the coroner's office. Maybe not just anyone in the coroner's office, but someone who will be able to tell her what she needs to know while we're waiting.

Like all the benches in the green area, this one faces the river and the bridge. And of course I can see the stone support, even though it's too far away to actually see the blood. I close my eyes and try to put everything out of my mind. I'm sure now that I've made a big mistake in coming here.

"That's it then," Courtney is saying.

I come back to where I am. "That's what then?"

"Sam wasn't wearing a cross when his body was recovered. We're going to have to recover that cross, or whatever it is stuck in the wall. Then, if you're sure you can identify it without doubt that it *is* Sam's cross, you have to tell the coroner."

I can see Courtney has an idea, but she seems reluctant to share it. "Janika, you're not going to like to hear this, but I think we can prove that Sam didn't take his own life, with or without the bloodstain on top of the parapet."

Not going to like to hear it? I can't think of anything better – apart from hearing that the body has been misidentified, and Sam is still alive somewhere. What on earth does Courtney mean? "Go on, share."

She's shaking her head. "I can't. The police need to retrieve whatever it is from the wall. If I'm right, it's too gruesome to even think about."

I put my hand to my mouth. I suddenly realise exactly what she's thinking. "Oh, Courtney, that's absolutely horrible. Horrible, horrible, horrible." I'm feeling sick at the thought, and lean over the grass, actually retching.

Courtney pats me gently on the back, presumably thinking that will help. "But at least it will bring in a verdict of murder rather than suicide," she says.

She's right, of course, and I owe it to Sam to get the right verdict, irrespective of getting his life insurance and some sort of payment from the police for death while on duty.

"I'm going back to the police station to make a full report," she tells me. "But I'll see you back home first."

That sounds crazy. "We need to retrieve the cross quickly. If we can find a long stick and fix a metal hook on the end, we can do it ourselves. I know it's small, but there might be part of someone else's fingerprint on it."

I can see Courtney shaking her head. "That won't be good enough," she says. "It needs to be recovered officially by the police. If you take it to the coroner, assuming it *is* Sam's cross, what proof do you have that it was stuck between the stones on the bridge? You might have found it at home and pretended to find it here, to influence the coroner."

It's a good thing I'm not in the police, making a dreadful blunder like that. I shake my head and lean forward again, my stomach contents coming up into my throat. Do I hope it is Sam's cross? Of course I do. Do I want a verdict of murder by person or persons unknown?

Of course I do. It's just that I can't handle the thought of Sam being dangled by his ankles long enough to slip the cross over his head to stick it in the wall in the hope that it will be discovered, before being released to crash head-first onto the ground below.

Was Sam gagged? Probably not, if they were trying to extract information out of him. That's grim.

I look into Abi's eyes. I've obviously been telling this account while I've been reliving those events of six months ago in my mind. "And that's when I decided to become a private detective," I tell her.

Chapter 4

"A private detective," Abi says in surprise. "A private investigator? What, *here*?"

I'm taken aback. "Is that a problem?"

Abi isn't laughing, but I can see she's thinking. Probably my story has affected her, so she doesn't feel that laughing would be appropriate. I'm glad.

"The Button Up Detective Agency," she says quietly.

That really takes the wind out of my sails. I did my homework carefully before thinking of moving here. I've been imagining I'll be the only private detective in town. "I didn't know about them," I say.

Abi still isn't laughing, but she's giving a sort of secret smile. "There isn't one. Not yet. But I was saying recently that when Mr Jennings leaves, it would be great to have a detective agency above here, and we could call it the Button Up Detective Agency. I thought I could help out in my free time. I have this totally undeserved reputation for being nosy, but I've helped untangle a few mysteries. I'm also good at cryptic crosswords, but I'm not sure what sort of use that would be to you."

"The Button Up Detective Agency?" I shake my head. "I'm calling it the Ja-Jo Detective Bureau. From my name. But if you're thinking of starting your own agency, I don't want to cramp you."

Abi takes a deep breath. "Not *me*, Janika. Do you *really* want to rent this apartment? If you do, you're welcome to use the name. I'm never going to use it. It's just something I thought up. I wouldn't mind helping out though. For free, of course. I don't know much about detective work, but maybe there will be times when two brains are better than one, if you ever want to discuss your work in confidence."

I'm not sure I want any help, but the time might come. I'm also quite good at cryptic crosswords. So was Sam. We used to leave notes for each other, just for fun. Things like, "Disney hour reinvention," for "Your dinner is in the oven." I smile to myself as I remember that one, and once again I can see Sam puzzling over it when he got back late from work one day, but he solved it quickly. I think the smell of hot food helped him crack it. I can't see where that ability will fit in with the work of a private investigator. The main thing is to establish the business first and get clients.

The Button Up Detective Agency? It sounds good. But is it better than Ja-Jo?

"People would know where to find you," Abi says. "The Button Up coffee shop is well known in town. Well, quite well known. Especially amongst workers in the offices." She stops for a moment. "You'll have to meet my husband Danny. He's a junior solicitor with Branks, Davis & Waters. They're a large legal firm in Jubilee Street. I'm sure they could use you. Well, I can't guarantee it of course. What sort of work are you planning to do here? That is, if you really want this apartment. No pressure, but please say yes. I'd just love it if you came, Janika!"

It all sounds a bit too easy. Now that I finally have Sam's life insurance money and a generous payout by the police for death while on duty, I can easily afford it. Unfortunately, I was evicted and our furniture was repossessed before the coroner officially ruled a verdict of murder by person or persons unknown, and I can't stay with Sam's friends in Brevelstone much longer. So I definitely need somewhere to live.

Abi seems to notice my hesitation, and mistakes it for uncertainty. "I'd love you to have it, Janika. And I know Danny would, too. The monthly rent is only a suggestion. How about if we give you a generous discount?"

Just as long as you don't interfere too much, I'm thinking, but I'm definitely not going to say it. I've done a residential course and distance learning with exams over the past six months to get my qualifications, plus a comprehensive course of self defence. I don't have a certificate for that, but I still have bruises as proof.

Anyone can be a private investigator in England, but to be taken seriously you need to have a couple of impressive certificates on the wall, and the backing of a reputable organisation. Plus, of course, the knowledge. I didn't realise all the potential pitfalls until I started the course.

It's easy to mess up and spoil a possible criminal investigation, or even a private one – like recovering Sam's gold cross by myself, without any witnesses. I'm not wearing that gold cross. I don't think it would be honest to do it. But I carry it with me everywhere in my bag.

I have a private investigator's license in the UK, issued by the Security Industry Authority, or SIA. It's not essential at the moment, but I suspect it will be soon, and I want to be ahead in the game when the time comes.

"I definitely want to take it, Abi," I hear myself saying. "And if you're serious about the name of the Button Up Detective Agency, that sounds better than my suggestion. It really does. The rent is fine. Honestly it is. I've already kitted myself out with an advanced bug detector, surveillance cameras and listening equipment. And quite a few more things. It cost several grand altogether, but it's all paid for. I want to start off as a fully fledged detective. I've got more than enough put aside to do pro bono work until my name gets known. I'm even prepared to pay you for the name."

"We'll see about that," Abi says.

I'm not exactly sure what we'll see about. Presumably I'm paying the full rent and able to use the suggested name. That's fine with me.

"Come down and meet the gang," Abi says. "Melanie will be back with Liam. She went to pick him up from school. Melanie Donovan is the co-owner with me of Button Up. Button Up comes in putting our two surnames together."

"Button Donovan?"

That really makes Abi laugh. She seems to be getting over the traumatic account of my past. "She used to be called Melanie Upton. So, Button Up. But I'm now Wells, and she's Donovan, and as I've said to people before, the name of the coffee shop doesn't make sense now. But that's what it is, and that's what it always will be while Melanie and I are the owners. Just about everyone still thinks of me as Abi Button. It's not a problem." And she shrugs.

I'm not sure I feel ready to meet what she calls the gang. I want to get back to Brevelstone. The friends with whom I'm staying will be expecting me. Maybe I'll phone them and explain the good news that I've found the perfect location for my new venture. I will be the only private detective in a town where there's a large legal practice where it seems I already have one foot in the door. Well, tentatively in the door. How good is that!

I'm not really in the mood for meeting new people. Just reliving Sam's death has drained me of all energy, and I've not told Abi that the police haven't yet managed to track down Sam's killers. But that item of bad news can definitely wait.

Abi has a pleading look in her eyes, and I can tell she wants me to meet what she calls the gang down below. So I give in. Melanie seems a happy sort of person. I'm surprised to see that she's older than Abi – by a good ten years. She is also shorter than me, but obviously weighs more. A lot more. She introduces me to a small boy with ginger hair. Apparently it's her stepson, and he's called Liam.

Liam looks excited when he hears I'm a private detective. "Do you have a gun?" he asks enthusiastically. "Can I see it? Have you ever shot anyone?"

It seems almost cruel to disappoint him. "No gun," I

say. "Private detectives in England aren't allowed guns."

"Have you ever used one?"

I nod, so at least I'm able to satisfy him to a certain extent. "On a firing range in Poland. My father wanted me to learn, but it was a long time ago. Anyway, I'm not exactly an expert shot, and I don't need a gun here in England. I don't do dangerous work. You'd probably think it's all rather boring. I'm going to help trace people who have gone missing, and check up on people who are supposed to be behaving themselves at work, but might be stealing or spending their time doing something else."

"I suppose that's cool," he says, sounding slightly disillusioned. Then he smiles. "Do you know Sherlock Holmes?"

I nod. "Very well."

"Wow," Liam says, "you must be *very* old. Even older than Melanie. You don't look it."

"I mean I know the Sherlock Holmes *stories* well," I say.

Melanie bats the boy away playfully, and anyway Liam seems to be losing interest. What else am I planning to do in my new detective agency? Liam is too young to be told I may be asked to investigate straying partners, and it's not work I'm going to feel comfortable with. On the positive side, if it means stopping a husband or wife being betrayed and perhaps losing a large sum of money, I'll have to consider taking it on. But I don't want to do sneaky. Definitely not sneaky.

"Mystery shopping," I say. The coffee shop only has a couple of customers, and the young man, Pete Wilders, seems to be more than capable of sorting out their orders. He's also been joined by a young friend who also seems to be working here, but I don't know who she is. No doubt I'll be told soon enough.

"Mystery shopping?" Melanie asks. "Does someone *pay* you to go shopping? That sounds like my sort of work."

"They do," I tell her. "Haven't you ever wanted to complain about the service you get in a shop?"

Both Melanie and Abi nod vigorously.

"Well," I explain, "if the management at head office get a lot of complaints, they need someone to test out the shopping experience. Or maybe they just want it checked out anyway, even if there haven't been complaints. So a private detective gets called in to play the part of the customer. Perhaps playing the part of an awkward customer, and making a note of what happens. Small shops may suspect that someone is fiddling the sales, and pocketing some of the money. Or a supermarket till operator might be ringing things through at a reduced price for friends, or ringing an expensive item through on top of a cheap one, so only the bottom barcode gets read."

Young Liam has returned, probably in the hope of hearing something exciting connected with my work, and his reaction is predictable. "That *is* boring," is his contribution to the discussion.

I soon learn that the young girl is called Hayley, and she is also a student. She and Pete seem remarkably close, in all senses of the word. I smile to myself. Young love. Then a sudden jolt hits me as I recall my early experience of young love in Poland with Bruno, at the tender age of eighteen, and how it ended in tragedy. It's the chief reason I came back to England, much to my parents' displeasure.

Liam is told to scoot off and get himself a jam doughnut and take it into the stockroom and let the grown-ups talk business. Since the discussion is, in his words boring, he seems happy enough to go. So we three adults discuss the terms and conditions of the rental, and Abi says her husband has already drawn up the necessary lease. All he has to do is to fill in my name. And although she obviously feels embarrassed to be saying it, Abi tells me it will be necessary to check my financial status.

"No problem," I say. I've already anticipated that. The insurance and other payouts are safely banked. "I'll authorise you to contact my bank."

I didn't think I'd ever be saying that, after Sam died. Evicted and homeless, and no prospect of any income. The hairstylist job hadn't materialised, and no local salons were looking for stylists. Life certainly moved on when I turned amateur detective and spotted Sam's gold cross pushed tightly into the gap between the stones on the bridge, so ruling out suicide. I can only hope life will continue to move on now that I'm about to turn professional.

Chapter 5

I'm back home now in Brevelstone, where I've been living with Jezza and Rachel since Sam's death. They seem as excited as I am about the apartment above the coffee shop. I'm hoping it's not because they want to see me gone. No, I'm sure it's not that.

Jezza and Rachel were friends Sam knew when he was young. We met up with them after we were married and they invited us to church. Certainly something happened to Sam there, and he kept wanting to go. It annoyed me when he tried to explain what had happened, and we came to a compromise. I would go with him on Sundays, as long as he didn't talk to me about it. He said that was a fair deal, and I could tell church meant something more to him than just religion. Now, if it meant having Sam back, I'd go with him a hundred times a week!

Jezza and Rachel have turned out to be great friends, and they certainly didn't try preaching to me when I was at my most vulnerable. However, they said they were praying for me, and they did offer me great practical support, including making sure I still went to live with them in their large Victorian house when I was made homeless, even though Sam had died.

I keep forgetting I'm a widow. I'm not a widow who wears black widow's weeds, or whatever mourning clothes are called nowadays. I didn't even wear black for Sam's funeral. I wanted to celebrate his life. Our life. I felt sure he wouldn't have wanted me wearing all black.

I wondered at the time if he was watching the funeral service from heaven. He was sure he was going there, and I know he wanted me to join him when the time came. I don't think I've ever been good enough to deserve a place. Not that Sam was perfect in every way, but he was a great husband. But he definitely seemed sure about having a place. I hope for his sake it wasn't wishful thinking.

I'm thinking back to the police investigation that Courtney helped reopen, just when the case seemed closed and the coroner was about to pronounce a damning verdict. I'm picturing it all now.

Courtney has just phoned Detective Inspector Dickinson to explain what we've just discovered. I don't think he sounded that impressed, but he's promised to pass the news on to the Chief Inspector. He must have done it immediately, because Courtney has just got a call to tell her to stay where she is, and guard the scene.

She winks at me. "I don't know what DI Dickinson said, but something is definitely happening. Forensics are on their way."

They probably don't want to think one of their own has taken their own life. They'd much rather have a crime to investigate. I'm hoping they're not doing it just for the sake of an exciting job, but to get justice. I'm sure that's what Courtney means. Courtney tells me I can leave her now, but I want to stay.

"Just as long as you keep well back," she says. "I'm sure you realise just how important it is to let the team get on with their work."

That rather disappoints me. I want to tell them my theory about the pendant, but I guess it's time to keep my mouth shut. Courtney understands the situation probably better than I do. But it will be interesting to watch the crime scene team in action.

Detective work can be exciting at times, although Sam assured me there are a lot of boring, routine tasks involved, and plenty of paperwork. Courtney has already explained to the forensic team about the need to recover the gold cross, and they seem to be going about it in a very methodical way. I can't believe I was even thinking about getting a long bamboo cane from the hardware store and a metal screw hook, and fishing it up myself.

No, that clearly isn't the way. The team have brought a long extending ladder. Courtney explains to me that the first thing they need to do is take detailed photographs of the cross to show exactly where it is, and how firmly it's fixed in the wall. After all, she points out, it might just have snagged there while Sam fell.

I point out that the leather cord would have broken if that was the case, but Courtney says that if the placing of the cross is going to be used as evidence of murder, every little detail counts. I guess she's right. Yes, there's certainly a lot of detail needed in detective work if evidence is going to be used to prove the case. I'm wondering if I can follow in Sam's footsteps, but not in the police force. Maybe privately. I give myself a mental slap on the wrist.

Stop daydreaming, Janika!

I can't believe how long this is taking. While the cross is being recovered, a young woman wearing white coveralls and a mask is painstakingly scraping what looks like the bloodstain from the concrete slab on top of the parapet. She looks at me, and seems to be smiling behind the mask.

"Well spotted," she says.

I'm about to ask why it got overlooked the first time, but I guess that everyone thought it was suicide, because of that phone call. Right, I decide, I'm going to play detectives myself. I'm going to track that woman down. Not that I have a clue how to do it.

If I believed in prayer, then I would have to think that some higher power had just read my thoughts and decided to answer them instantly.

"What's going on here?" a middle aged woman asks. She has a camera round her neck and a recorder in her hand. "We got a tipoff from a member of the public who was passing."

"Sorry, no press," Courtney tells her quickly. "This is an ongoing investigation. We'll tell you more later."

"This is where the man jumped, isn't it?" The woman must be a reporter. She has her camera already switched on and ready for action.

"Sorry," Courtney says again, "I must ask you to move on."

The woman is already taking photographs, and she leans over the parapet a bit further down the bridge and spots the ladder. Without a word she goes to the start of the bridge and is obviously going down to the concrete area where the crime team ladder is resting.

I make an instant decision. I make it before I can even run it through my mind to see if it's sensible. "Hold on," I call, hurrying after her. "I'm Janika Jones. It was my husband who ... died here."

Died here? That probably describes it best. I'm not going to use the word murder yet, and certainly not suicide.

The reporter stops instantly. She even has the cheek to whip the camera up and take a photograph of me. I'm still grieving, and can do without the publicity, but I guess that's the press for you.

At the moment the reporter seems in a dilemma. Should she talk to me, or get a photograph of one of the crime scene team at the top of the ladder trying to recover the gold cross? She manages to do both, beckoning to me to walk down with her onto the area of concrete.

Now I'm wondering if I'm about to do the right thing. If the phone call from the so-called witness was genuine, and Sam was really on his own and about to jump, then the coroner will definitely rule out murder, irrespective of what the crime scene team are finding at this moment. My only hope is that she was confused by what she saw, and there were actually two people there, not just one. Or, more likely, the call was a hoax from one of the murderers, to stop a police investigation.

The reporter introduces herself as Morgan, and she works for the local newspaper. I know it. It's mostly advertisements, and only comes out on a Friday. It's Thursday now, so hopefully it hasn't already been put to bed, or whatever the expression is.

I explain about the so-called witness who made the phone call, which is news to Morgan. I can see her eyes light up. She's managed to get an exclusive. Now, of course, I'm wondering if I'm giving away potential evidence, but I don't really care. It seems that the police have already made up their mind it was suicide, so what's wrong with me telling about the phone call? I haven't been told to keep it secret.

I notice that her small digital recorder is running, if the small red light is anything to go by. Morgan even takes another picture of me with the bridge and the ladder in the background. What do I care!

Morgan smiles as I tell her what I want. And she nods, holding the small digital recorder that still has the red light on, and says, "A plea for the woman to come forward? The police haven't asked us to do this, but we'll definitely get it in the paper tomorrow. I guarantee it."

"The thing is, I suspect my husband was murdered, but please don't say that at the moment, not while the police are still investigating. If the call was genuine, why didn't the woman leave her name?"

Morgan is shaking her head. "There might be all sorts of reasons why she's chosen to remain anonymous. She might be married and was visiting her lover. She would have known her phone wasn't registered. Do you see what I mean?"

"I do," I say. "I definitely do, but if it *was* a genuine call, and she doesn't mind coming forward, she might have seen something happening that she didn't realise was important. I'll be frank with you, Morgan. The crime scene team are here now because I believe there's evidence that Sam was murdered."

I'm wondering whether to tell her about the cross, which the woman on the ladder has just recovered and is putting in a see-through evidence bag. Morgan has spotted what's happening, and hurries forward. Perhaps I've told her too much. If this is in the press, perhaps the coroner will dismiss the whole case supporting murder. Well, we'll have to see what happens.

Chapter 6

Jezza and Rachel bring me back to the present by asking if I'd like something to drink after my office hunting adventure. I opt for tea. I know I've got to stop reliving the past. But the past is an important part of my life.

"So when will you be moving in?" Rachel asks. "Please stay here as long as you want. Opening a detective agency is a big move, Janika."

Don't I know it! "Abi's husband is a solicitor, and he's drawn up a tenancy agreement. I've not signed it yet, and Abi has to change the furniture in the living accommodation. Fortunately, she hasn't done it yet, because she was going to refurbish the office with brand-new stuff. What's there now is perfect. It will look as though I've been in business for years, and know exactly what I'm doing."

Yes, that's going to be a borderland deception, but I'm not going to tell any clients about this being my first job, unless of course they ask. It's scary. Definitely scary, but I have more than enough money now. Then, when I've made my fortune, I can purchase my own property. The immediate payouts were good, but not generous enough to do that straight away. The police compensation will be paid out over a number of years.

"I can pay the rent and survive for at least a year, even if I don't get any income," I explain. "Abi is an old school friend of mine, so I'm getting a friendly reduction on the rent."

That's not exactly true. Yes, I'm getting a friendly reduction on the rent, but I could never call Abi an old school friend. When she told me about laughing at my mother's new Citroen 2CV, I could hardly remember it. But I can remember it now. It wasn't just Abi, but it certainly hurt. After that, I insisted on walking to school, and when it was wet, my mother dropped me off a couple of roads away so I could walk the last part and arrive at school without being mocked.

I've really taken to Abi. If I hadn't been such a mouse at school we might have become friends back then. She has a dry sense of humour, and is certainly more considerate than the Abi Button schoolgirl I knew. That's probably what happens when people grow up. Everyone changes, but not always for the better. Anyway, I already feel comfortable with Abi and Melanie, and Pete and Hayley. There's definitely something going on with Pete and Hayley.

Little ginger haired Liam Donovan is quite a character. He wanted to show me some magic, but his mother told him not to bother me because I have a lot on my mind. I think she meant my decision about taking the office and apartment above the coffee shop, and not my loss of Sam. I'm not sure she even knew about that. Well, she will now, because Abi will definitely have told her. I hope it doesn't lead to embarrassment next time we meet. People don't know what to say when they learn about Sam.

"Sorry, Rachel, what did you say?"

Rachel reminds me she has just asked if I would like something to eat now, or would I like to wait until they eat at seven. I'm not at all hungry. The day has exhausted me. Am I really about to start a detective agency called the Button Up Detective Agency?

"Coffee?"

I shake my head vigorously. "Thanks, but not today. I had more than enough coffee at Button Up, and I'm so wound up about the move that I'll probably not sleep a wink tonight."

Rachel just smiles. She and Jezza have been great friends. As soon as they learnt of our financial problems – that's Sam's as well as mine – they've been bricks. They've not had money to spare, and if they'd offered us a loan we wouldn't have taken it, but they've made sure I've not been made homeless. And before Sam's sudden death, we were both going to live here with them, while we sorted out our future – however long it took.

I've told Rachel and Jezza about the lovely old furniture in the office, and the not so lovely old furniture in the living accommodation. I'm keen to get started as soon as I can, but I think it's going to be a couple of weeks until things are fixed there. Abi says she wants to fit new units in the small kitchen, and says I can rest assured that she's already onto it. She's a real ball of fire, that girl!

"I hope I'll be able to take most of my stuff with me," I tell Jezza and Rachel. "All the furniture belonged to the landlord, and apart from some treasured possessions from our past, and books, there's not much here anyway. Is it okay if I leave some of it behind? For now, I mean."

"Janika," Rachel says, giving me a hug, "we'll do whatever we can to help you. Please don't worry. Everything is safe here until you need it."

"I'm going to need to change my car before I start work," I tell them. "My old Nissan Micra is hardly going to impress clients if I turn up at their home or place of work to discuss a potential case."

The Micra and the laptop are only two things of any value that the bailiffs couldn't take. They belong to my father, even though he's never used them. Fortunately I had the documents as proof when they raided the house.

Jezza is laughing and shaking his head. "Are you sure you want to be a private detective?" he asks with a grin.

I don't get it. "I don't mind old office furniture. It's impressive – but my old silver Nissan Micra? That's not going to go down well. I just hope no one notices me in it."

"Exactly," Jezza says. "No one will notice you *or* the car. Isn't that perfect if you want to carry out surveillance?"

I'm feeling so stupid. There's me, trained and qualified, and I'm thinking of buying a new car. What, a bright red supercar? But I'm not going to let Jezza off easily. "Not so unnoticeable if it keeps breaking down and leaving a trail of smoke in its wake."

Of course, Rachel is now in on the act. "Then get it fixed, Janika. Instead of spending the money on a new car, find someone to make it reliable and fast."

I'm having to laugh, mostly at my own stupidity. "Brilliant idea, Rachel. Thanks for raising it, Jezza. Abi told me she has a friend called Rupert Forrester who works in a local garage. I'll take it to him. But I'm not bothered about the speed. I'm going to be following people, assuming I get work, but I won't be doing high-speed chases."

It's good to have sensible friends – even ones who go to church! Yes, the little Nissan Micra will be perfect. It will blend in, as long as I get the dent and scrape in the passenger door fixed first. With damage like that, the little car would be easily identified if it kept popping up in various parts of town. Why wasn't that in the course I did? Maybe it's so obvious that it didn't need stating. We were told how to follow someone in a car without being noticed, and in my mind I've been picturing myself sitting in something fast, expensive and new.

My phone is ringing, and makes me jump. Fortunately, I've been able to retain my old number, even though I was temporarily cut off by the phone company for non-payment. I'm wondering which of my friends it is now. I look at the screen. It's Abi Wells.

"Hi," Abi says, "I've already arranged house clearance to get rid of the old stuff in the living accommodation. And I've ordered the necessary flatpack. My friends Alice and Rupert will help me and Danny put it all together, and we have a builder friend from church who's doing the decorating. Danny has the tenancy agreement, and if you can print it out yourself, I'll email it to you now as an attachment."

It's good I've managed to keep our laptop. Well, it's my laptop now, not Sam's as well. I still keep thinking of

Sam and me as an item, and I've been told I need to give it time. Probably several years. If ever. And I'm not sure it's something I ever want to get over. No way will I be finding someone to take Sam's place in my life.

The bailiffs took the printer, but I can use Rachel and Jezza's for now. So I'm looking forward to perusing and signing the tenancy agreement, knowing it will be more than fair. Abi is someone I feel I can trust. Although I've not met Danny, I have no doubts I'll sign it, which means I can set up business within the next two weeks.

Hooray!

Really? My laptop is open and my email pings. It's not only the tenancy agreement from Abi, but pictures of the flatpack furniture she's chosen, and the kitchen units. There will be a small fridge freezer, and a sink unit with an adjoining worktop with an overhead cupboard. Under the worktop are pull-out drawers for my groceries. And that's it. Just those few things will fill the tiny kitchen, but I know I'm going to love it. Especially knowing that the welcoming coffee shop is immediately below.

Rupert is apparently keen to inspect my Nissan Micra and give me a quote as soon as I move in. It seems I already have friends in the town that holds some unpleasant childhood memories. At the moment I'm glad I'm going back there to live and work. I hope I won't regret it later.

Chapter 7

I was right about not being able to get to sleep. I'm lying in bed staring at the ceiling. There's light coming through the curtains from the streetlight a little way down the road, but that's not the reason. I keep thinking of Sam.

I hope I'm not heading for a breakdown. I've been assured that it's perfectly normal to feel like this after such a sudden and totally unexpected loss, but my mind is certainly buzzing in a way that doesn't feel right. I'm reliving the results of the findings at the crime scene.

It was definitely a crime scene, and officially declared as such. However, the coroner didn't seem to take the report for granted. No woman came forward from the appeal in the newspaper, or subsequently from an appeal on the local radio, but that didn't seem a significant part of his conclusion. I realised that the police weren't there to present the case one way or the other, although they were allowed to state their findings. It was the coroner who took all the evidence into account before making his decision.

I couldn't afford him, but I didn't tell my solicitor I was broke when I signed him on. Courtney had advised me to get a solicitor, and this one was certainly sharp. He reinforced the police report that there was *no* way that Sam's gold cross and unbroken leather cord could have ended up where it did, without being placed there manually. The coroner then suggested that perhaps I had placed it there, but my solicitor quickly pointed out that – with all due respect – the suggestion was ludicrous. I would not have been able to place a ladder there without being noticed, and no one had reported it. Also, a ladder that tall would have needed at least two people to handle it.

I think the coroner wanted to be absolutely sure he was making the right decision. A lot depended on it. Not just my own peace of mind, of course, but there was a question of a large life insurance payout and compensation from the police.

I'm sure that without the intervention of my solicitor the coroner might have given an open verdict, which of course would be totally unsatisfactory. Eventually, and I got the feeling it was reluctantly, he ruled that Sam's death was murder, by person or persons unknown.

I fluttered my eyelids after the inquest and explained to my solicitor that – with all due respect – I wouldn't be able to pay him until the insurance money came through. That really brought him to life, and he explained that the situation was certainly unusual, but if I wanted him to pursue the insurance company and the police compensation, he would be glad to do so for a small commission. He didn't explain how small the commission was going to be, but I could call in the next day to sign a contract. I found it a great relief to have him on my side. The man was sharp, but also a total softy.

It looks as though Danny Wells is kind, too, because

he's not inserted any nasty clauses into the tenancy agreement. I'm hoping he'll be able to get me some detective work through the solicitors' office, but nothing too tricky to begin with. Just something that pays well!

I have to get in touch with my parents in Poland to tell them about the office and living apartment, and give them what will be my new address. They came over for the funeral, but we more or less lost contact again after Sam's death. Not that we've had much contact anyway. My mother kept warning me that I was foolish to be marrying a policeman instead of Bruno, because of the dangers. Instead of showing sympathy when Sam was killed, all she could say was, "I told you so," and subsequently she's been no help. Perhaps when she knows I've made something of my life when I start the detective agency, the rift will be healed. Not that it will bring Sam back.

Foregoing Rachel's offer of coffee doesn't seem to have helped me sleep. I'm still wide awake, wondering who these person or persons unknown are. Well, obviously if I knew who they were, they wouldn't be person or persons unknown. And that's the problem.

Courtney has become quite a good friend, and she's warned me several times against trying to track them down. She says the police are onto it, and that's all she's allowed to say. Well, I hope they find them soon. I'm worried they might find me first, wanting to know if Sam shared any incriminating details with me. Maybe even keeping some sort of notebook, or coded file on our laptop. I've not seen one yet, and I'm doubtful there is one. Surely Sam's records would be at work. But if I do find anything, Courtney will be the first person to know.

Even though Sam didn't share anything with me, the person or persons unknown won't know that. I get this nightmarish picture of being hung over the bridge by my ankles, by two men demanding to know what Sam has told me. I'm wondering why I would bother to tell them anything. They're going to let me drop, anyway. They won't want me reporting them. I imagine the same thought occurred to Sam. I'm not imagining myself hanging there now, but I'm seeing Sam in his last moments. I wish I couldn't keep thinking about these things. Thoughts like this are at their worst in the night.

Whether Sam told anything or not I have no idea, but that gold cross certainly didn't bring him any luck. Maybe that's not why he wore it. I'm feeling sad that he never talked about it with me, probably because we got into arguments. Getting into an argument is the last thing I'd do now – if he could come back.

Of course, he won't come back. I don't believe in ghosts. I wonder if Sam is preparing a place for me in heaven. I heard that somewhere. No, I'm pretty certain it was Jesus who said it. He told his followers not to worry, because he was preparing a place for them in heaven. Really? Well, Sam certainly believed it.

<><><><>

I slept a bit during the night. I can remember a few of my dreams, and they weren't as bad as my waking thoughts. Perhaps I need to get some professional help. Of course, the sooner I can get to work and have something to occupy my mind, the better I'm likely to feel.

It's Saturday now, and Jezza and Rachel aren't going to work. Rachel suggests they take me to lunch at Button Up. It seems I've made the coffee and pastries at Button Up sound extremely attractive. If Abi is amenable I'll show them the office, just to make sure they agree with me that the traditional furniture will give my clients the right impression. And they might as well see the living accommodation, even though it is all rather cramped. But if it was good enough for an elderly accountant, I'm sure it's going to be good enough for little me.

I need to phone Abi.

"Abi, Janika here. I've signed the tenancy agreement. I'm happy to pay the full deposit. As I explained yesterday, I have adequate funds to start the business. I'd rather we got off on a professional footing, even though we're friends."

Are we friends? Am I taking something for granted here?

"Come any time, Janika. This is my Saturday to be on duty. Melanie and I take turns for the Saturday work. Pete and Hayley will be here. They are fascinated by the thought of having a private investigator living above the coffee shop. They've hardly stopped talking about you. Good things, of course."

I can't help wondering what they've been saying, but thankfully whatever it is, it seems to have been okay. "I know it's not properly furnished yet, but is it all right if I bring my friends to look round the apartment? I told you about Jezza and Rachel. They'll drive me over, and I can drop the signed tenancy agreement off at the same time.

As soon as you've signed it and given me a copy, I'll do a bank transfer with the deposit and the first month's rent, to start whenever the apartment is ready. No pressure, but I'm *dying* to get my feet under that old desk."

Not a good choice of word.

Chapter 8

While I've been talking to Abi, a tone on my phone has told me there's an incoming call. It's a number I recognise, and I'm certainly not going to tell Abi to get off the line. The call could be bad news.

With everything arranged with Abi for a visit at lunchtime, and a complimentary lunch offered at Button Up for me, Jezza and Rachel, I go into the garden to return the call. I don't want to be overheard. It's Mr Mulligan, the cruel, cruel landlord who evicted me, even in the middle of the trauma of Sam's death. Well, perhaps not cruel, because he understandably wanted an income on his investment. I could afford the monthly rent now, but no way do I want to live there on my own. So if his new tenants have also defaulted on their rent, and he's begging me to come back, he's in for a disappointment.

"Mrs Jones," he snaps, "you've done a very serious thing. My tenants are absolutely furious. You're lucky they haven't gone to the police about it, although I have a good mind to go myself."

I shake my head. "Mr Mulligan, I've absolutely no idea what you're talking about."

"No, no, Mrs Jones, you're not going to get out of it that easily. I think it's disgraceful to spy on anyone. Was it you or was it your husband?"

"I've not been back near the place since the day I

left," I say. What on earth is the man talking about?

"I know your husband was with the police, but I didn't know he was some sort of pervert. Or was it your idea to keep an eye on whoever moved in next?"

"I'm sorry, Mr Mulligan, but I'm going to hang up. You're talking nonsense. I paid you the rent arrears three months ago when the insurance came through, and whatever your tenants are up to, please don't phone me about it. Understand?"

"Mrs Jones, my tenants reported a problem with the lights, and my electrician has been in there this morning to sort things out."

Mr Mulligan is making it sound as though it's my fault, but the lights were working perfectly when I left. Anyway, has it really taken six months for some electrical problem to show? I came here to live with Jezza and Rachel immediately after Sam's death. And now I'm getting the blame?

"I'm talking about the spy cameras and things," Mr Mulligan shouts. He sounds as though he's about to give himself a heart attack. I hope he doesn't have high blood pressure.

"I know I didn't leave anything behind," I tell him, trying to put on a voice that will calm him down.

"They weren't *left behind*, Mrs Jones. They were *hidden* in the ceiling light fittings in the living room and the main bedroom. Sneaky little cameras and microphones. Don't deny it. I've got them here in my hand. What's your explanation ... *pervert*?"

I know Sam didn't hide them. What would be the

point? Someone obviously got in during the day while we were living there, and hid them. Someone from the gang that eventually killed him? I feel violated that our private conversations were recorded. And not just conversations. A camera. *Cameras.* Suddenly I don't want to be a private detective checking up on people. The whole concept of private investigation sounds obscene.

But things are making sense. Sam was obviously being trailed by the gang. Even if they hadn't managed to tap his mobile phone, they would have been able to hear one side of every conversation he made at home. I'm sure he told me where he was going on the evening he was killed.

"Mr Mulligan, you have to take everything to the police at once. I think that stuff must have been put there by whoever killed Sam. Give me five minutes, and I'll tip them off at the station about what's happening. Please, this is important. Sam and I are not to blame, but the police might be able to track down the people who left the spy equipment."

There, that should let my old landlord calm down a bit. "You have to do it, Mr Mulligan. Please. The police will do a proper bug search. There might be more equipment that your electrician hasn't found. But whatever you do, don't do any more searching. Try not to handle anything. Put it all in a polythene sandwich bag and I'll phone you back."

"I'm not convinced it's nothing to do with you, Mrs Jones, or with your husband. Believe me, I'm seriously regretting ever having rented the property to the two of you."

I'm not going to respond to that. Anyway, he has a perfectly valid point. We got three months behind with the rent and he had to go to the bother of evicting us. We certainly put him to a lot of trouble.

I'm phoning Courtney. It's her day off, but she's listening to me, and clearly takes the discovery seriously. She's going to contact someone senior who's on duty and explain the situation to them. I give her Mr Mulligan's phone number, and she tells me I can leave the matter in her hands.

I'm glad I came out into the garden to take the call. This is a large old house with a large garden, and I know the neighbours won't be listening. I can just imagine how Jezza and Rachel would feel if there were bugs in this house.

A horrible panic runs through me. "Jezza, Rachel, come out here quickly. I've got something important to say."

They're coming out now, looking puzzled.

"That sounds like a serious call you've just received," Rachel says. "You look upset, Janika. Problem over your new apartment? We don't have to go today."

We go down to the end of the garden, and very quietly I explain about Mr Mulligan and the surveillance equipment.

"That's nasty," Rachel says, and I signal to her to keep her voice down.

"Rachel, Jezza, have you had any trades people in the house that you didn't expect?"

I can see they've caught on to what I'm thinking. Rachel looks at Jezza and they shake their heads. They go out to work Monday to Friday, and I've been away some of the time on my residential private investigators course since I've been living here.

I've always felt their front door lock isn't particularly secure, and there's no house alarm. However, the latch was secure enough to trap me outside when I first moved here. I was on my own and went to get something from my car, and the door blew shut behind me. I had no idea how to pick a lock, and I still don't. So I had to phone Rachel at work, and she kindly popped back to let me back in.

Naturally, from then on I've always made sure I have a key with me, even if I'm only going outside for a few seconds. What I want in my new apartment is a lock that needs a key to go out as well as in when the door closes and latches itself automatically. If I don't have the key, I can't leave the premises. Simple. Locking myself out will be one embarrassment I'm never going to face again.

Jezza is examining the lock. "It doesn't look damaged, but that doesn't mean someone hasn't managed to get in while we're out," he says. He's looking at Rachel. "Any thoughts?"

I'm probably panicking about nothing. Whether they know if anyone got in or not, the main thing is to discover if there are any hidden bugs. And I've got the equipment to do it.

"Stay out here," I say, taking command. "I'm going to do a sweep. We're not leaving for Button Up until I know your house is clear. I'm so sorry, this must be such a worry to you."

"I hope there's nothing in the bathroom," Rachel says.

"Or in our bedroom," Jezza adds.

I'm hoping there's nothing in my own ensuite bathroom. Anyway, I need to get on with it, either to set my own mind at rest or to give *all* of us reason to panic.

"I can't seriously believe anyone has bugged your house," I say. I hope they believe me. If the gang think Sam had passed information on to me, they might think I'm discussing it with my friends. Or they might hope to see me in my bedroom poring over a notebook belonging to Sam and then tucking it under the mattress – for them to retrieve when the house is empty. Of course, I don't have any sort of notebook that Sam left behind, although I do seem to remember him writing stuff down somewhere, but I wasn't really paying attention.

"If there *are* bugs," Jezza asks, raising his voice slightly more than I like, "will someone know you're searching for them?"

"The bugs probably send a signal to some nearby sensor that records video and conversation. There won't be somebody wearing headphones hiding in the bushes. I'll start the sweep now."

Of course Jezza insists on coming with me, which means Rachel does as well. I practised sweeping for bugs on the residential course, but searching for bugs hidden by the course leader isn't the same as doing it seriously. On the course, I'd been thinking it would be fun doing it for real, but the fact is it's a worry. Supposing there really *are* bugs? Video as well as sound.

My bug detector is fully charged and one of the most expensive models on the market. It will find radio transmitters of every possible frequency, but it won't find static recorders that don't actually transmit a signal over the air. But I can't imagine there will be any like that here. But it will find concealed cameras. Even cameras with a tiny pinhole lens.

Permanent spy bugs usually run off the house electricity, probably from tapping a cable in the ceiling. Some transmit a video and audio signal 24/7, and others need regular access to the recording medium to replace it. Most likely a memory card. I'm fairly convinced people haven't been coming and going regularly to this house. And even if there are bugs, whoever planted them probably gave up listening to them ages ago.

I'm starting in the hallway with my bug detector, the equipment automatically sweeping through every possible frequency. There's a signal on the detector screen and from the speaker, but not from a source close at hand. All sorts of domestic equipment emits radio signals, including televisions. So I ask Jezza and Rachel to hurry through the house and check that everything electronic is switched off, even the digital alarm clock in their bedroom.

I'm still picking up the signal. It seems to be coming from the dining room or the kitchen. It only takes a few seconds to pinpoint the source to the ceiling in the dining room. There is another camera and microphone bug in the kitchen, and another in the sitting room ceiling.

I whisper to my two friends not to speak, but beckon to them to follow me up the stairs. To their relief, and mine, their bedroom and the main bathroom are both free. But to my alarm, there's something in my bedroom ceiling light fitting. Snooping on people like this is a disgusting practice. Whatever made me think I wanted to be a private detective with a box full of advanced bugs?

I need to think of a new career. Perhaps go back to hairdressing, if I can get a job. I'm going to phone Abi Wells and tell her I'm sorry, but I won't be bringing the signed tenancy agreement.

Chapter 9

As we go back into the garden to discuss the next step, I'm starting to think more rationally. According to the law in the UK, I'm not allowed to enter private property and place bugs without permission. I can do it if the owner of the property, such as an office, requests me to do it, but I can't break the law by trespassing.

There's no way I could consider taking on an assignment to place bugs in a house like Jezza and Rachel's, assuming I didn't know them. But, more importantly, Jezza and Rachel could ask me to plant them, to keep an eye on the cleaner – or perhaps someone who was a carer for their elderly mother, if they had one living here. And that would be fine.

So perhaps it's a bit premature to be phoning Abi and cancelling that lovely office and small living apartment. Instead, I phonc Courtney and explain what I've found. I tell her that now their cover is blown, whoever planted them may well be aware that I'vc dctccted the bugs. And there might be bugs I've not managed to find. What does she suggest?

No one can expect to kill a member of the police force and find they are no longer being hunted. This case is still high priority. Courtney seems to be fully on top of the job. She's going to get the team that's on their way to

Mr Mulligan's house to come straight to mine. Mr Mulligan has already handled the bugs extensively, but when I assure her I haven't attempted to remove anything, she's excited by the prospect of finding fingerprints or perhaps DNA.

Five minutes after we've spoken, one of the crime scene detectives phones me and says they'll be over immediately, with a strong warning not to touch anything. She probably doesn't know about my training, and even if she does, it's not going to be as impressive as hers. So I bite my tongue and tell her we'll wait until the team arrives, and I promise I definitely *won't* touch anything.

Things move surprisingly quickly, and the leader, a woman probably in her fifties with a very commanding voice and steel grey hair pulled back into a bun, asks if we can possibly leave the team alone for a few hours.

"But Janika is an experienced ——"

"Don't worry, Rachel," I say quickly. I know she's about to explain that I'm a trained detective, but I'm not experienced in any way at all.

I smile. "Sam Jones was my husband, and he told me a bit about detecting, and I've been training to do some private investigation work. That's why I had the scanner." It's just as well to explain what's going on, without claiming any superior expertise.

I tell the team leader where I found the bugs, and I even have the decency to say I might have missed some, and their team may well find more.

She smiles, and I think we're sort of friends now. Anyway, it's thanks to me that she's here at all.

Within a few minutes we are more or less shooed out of the house, and politely told not to return until the evening. Is that all right? And do we have spare keys for the front door so they can lock up when they leave?

I get the impression that we *have* to go, whether it's all right or not. The team has work to do. Rachel asks if it's all right if we grab a few things, and the team leader says that's fine – as long as we don't speak a word. I get the impression we've already given the game away by doing the search, but then if we hadn't been looking, no one would be any the wiser about the bugs. It's just that I think the team leader is the sort of person who finds fault with everyone, and I'm feeling rather sorry for the rest of the team.

I'm standing in the front garden, waiting for Jezza and Rachel, and I can hear a car drawing up. To my surprise it's Courtney Jacobs, the Detective Constable who has been such a help to me so far. She comes across and explains that she was just following up on my phone call, and she's glad to see that the crime team have arrived.

"Is DI Dickinson coming, too?" I ask. It seems rather odd that a detective constable has come, and not the detective inspector who's in charge of the investigation.

Courtney is shaking her head. "The forensic team will report back to him, and I'm only here out of courtesy."

"Any updates on the investigation you can share? I take it you'll still be searching Mr Mulligan's house as well as collecting the bugs he's just found."

"I wish there was news," Courtney says. "We're following a few leads, but nothing major yet. This isn't the work of a small town drug dealer. This is something major. International. I'd love to share, but please don't ask me to tell you anything more."

I just nod. Jezza and Rachel still haven't appeared, and the silence between me and Courtney is starting to grow embarrassingly long. I eventually break it by asking, "How is DI Dickinson's family?" I remember Courtney saying there was some sort of problem. Perhaps I shouldn't be asking the question. It's no business of mine.

Courtney shakes her head but says nothing for a moment. Then she says, "We're not quite sure what's happening. He won't discuss his family life at the station. He has two kids in their early teens. His wife has left him and taken the kids. I've no idea why. We all thought he was quite a family man."

I think back to my own time in Poland when I nearly walked out on my parents. But I was in my early twenties.

"I'm sorry to hear that, Courtney. I won't say anything to him about it. Anyway, I've got to go. Jezza and Rachel are about to leave. We've been thrown out of the house." I laugh. "Well, not exactly thrown out, but told to keep out of the way for the rest of the day. Anyway, thanks for coming. It's good to keep contact with people Sam worked with."

Courtney laughs. "Don't think you've seen the last of me. Craidlea is still in the Brevelstone CID area."

"Great," I say. "Be sure to find some excuse to call in."

Thirty minutes later we're on our way to meet Abi, and are certainly not travelling in silence. We're making up for the time we weren't allowed to talk at the house. There's a lot of conjecture about who could have planted the bugs, and even whether it's going to be safe to return.

I'm really regretting taking up the offer of accommodation with Jezza and Rachel. It seems I've brought trouble with me. So when were the bugs placed in the house? Did someone plant them the moment Sam and I agreed to take up Sam's friends' offer of accommodation?

That makes sense. What possible reason could there be to check up on *me* living there without Sam? I'm starting to feel a bit better about it. I guess the forensic team will get some idea of when the bugs were hidden. I certainly hope so, and I try to comfort Jezza and Rachel with that reassuring thought.

The car journey to Button Up takes just over an hour. Rachel who is driving seems to be familiar with the small town, and I only have to give her directions to Button Up as we approach the centre.

Although the coffee shop is a little distance from the main shops, parking is tricky. I remember Abi telling me there's parking round the back of Button Up that Melanie Donovan uses. Melanie isn't going to be in today, and Abi says she walks to work when the weather is fine. I know it's a bit cheeky, but I suggest to Rachel she gives it a go.

The space is empty. I realise that without the waste skips, there would probably be room for two small cars. I'm not sure what can be done about the skips, but it would be great to have a permanent parking slot available for my little Nissan Micra when I move here.

We are rather late for lunch, but I phoned Abi before setting out and explained the situation, and said we would stop off on the way to get something to eat. She explained that food is served until they close just before six, so as long as we could hold out, we were welcome to eat there. And the offer of a free lunch for my guests was still valid.

I'm delighted to see that Jezza and Rachel take to Abi. In a few minutes they're talking together like old friends, even discussing their own churches. Young Pete has Hayley with him, and they start to prepare our various panini and toasties with side salad while we talk to Abi.

Pete Wilders seems to have a special interest in detection work, and he leaves Hayley to finish preparing our lunch order, and pulls up a chair to our table to hear the account of the hidden bugs. Abi tells him not to be so nosy, to which Pete rolls his eyes and retorts that that's a bit rich coming from her!

Pete is telling us how he and Hayley trailed an Italian conman, and apparently the two of them solved a major crime after tricking the man into letting Pete get his fingerprints.

Abi is smiling, and she tells us there's a bit more to it than that, but Melanie has a lot to thank Pete for. I guess we're going to hear more about it later, but Hayley calls Pete across to help serve up our late lunch.

There are several other customers in the coffee shop, but we're crowded around a small table in the corner that's out of earshot. Just as we are about to eat, a man in his thirties wearing an impressive slate blue business suit enters Button Up and makes his way straight to our table.

Abi introduces him as her husband Danny who has to work in the office today, even though it's a Saturday. So this is the famous junior solicitor – lawyer – who is going to help me make my fortune. Or not. He certainly dresses the part.

It's difficult eating and talking at the same time, and I can feel tomato ketchup around my lips from my cheese and ham panini. I wipe it away hastily with a Button Up printed napkin.

I'm hoping the conversation won't return to the bugs in my friend's house, or even the bugs in Mr Mulligan's house that Sam and I rented. I'm wondering how the search is going in Jezza and Rachel's house. The only person who is likely to let me know is Courtney.

Danny says he's interested to hear what I'll be doing, and he'll see if he can find me some work, but he's making no promises. I start to give a brief summary of what has led up to this, but it seems Abi has already given him the whole spiel. Well, it doesn't matter. It's not exactly a secret, and I'm glad Danny knows I'm properly qualified, even though I'm obviously green to the work.

I've got the signed tenancy agreement in my bag, and I hand it to Danny who quickly checks it. I notice he doesn't put it on the table, which has now got a bit messy. It's not me. I think Jezza pressed the ketchup bottle a bit too enthusiastically. But it doesn't matter. We are clearly among friends.

Abi is insisting we have coffee before looking at the apartment. Above the service counter there's a large clock shaped like a coffee cup and saucer. I'm guessing it was expensive. Although I'm anxious to show the apartment to my friends, I have to admit that the coffee here is so good that it's impossible to turn it down.

Abi asks if it's all right if she comes up with us. It can't be that she doesn't trust us, and she explains that she wants me to select the colour scheme for the walls which will be painted with an emulsion paint of my choosing. I've certainly not expected to be allowed that choice.

Abi then says I can choose the curtains in the bedsit, and what colour blind would I like for the office? It seems that when Abi inspected it after I left, she could see it was beyond repair.

"Abi," I say, "I'd much rather you did all the choosing. I might only be here for a year, if the private detective business doesn't work out. That's all I've signed the tenancy agreement for. I'd like you to make it some sort of universal colour that would suit anyone."

I don't think Abi is agreeing with me, so perhaps I ought to choose something safe. Certainly nothing outrageous. Anyway, an office should be a place of calm, so perhaps cream or magnolia on the walls? Or maybe pale green? I sigh. That's the problem with giving someone a choice. And what sort of curtains would I want in the living room-cum-bedroom? In other words, the bedsit.

I can envisage nervous clients asking if they can possibly use the toilet, and of course it will have to be the one in the living quarters, so the feeling of peace will have to extend there. I smile to myself. I've not realised setting up an office could be so much of a problem.

Anyway, whatever happens now, I have no doubts for my future. I, Janika Jones, recently widowed, will shortly be living and working here as the only private detective in town. How good is that! I'm just sorry that I've left a trail of bugs in my wake. Maybe I need to sweep this whole apartment before I move in.

Chapter 10

I've moved in at last. It feels strange to be in a different town, although I'm fairly familiar with parts of Craidlea because I grew up here.

The apartment looks quite homely now with my pictures on the wall, some photos of Sam and me in happier times, and one or two of my favourite ornaments. Soon I'll be able to bring everything I've left with Jezza and Rachel. I guess I really *have* started a new life now, and it scares me a bit.

Shortly before coming here to live, the reporter from the local newspaper who had interviewed me by Mill Bridge contacted me. She had my phone number, but didn't know I'd moved in with Jezza and Rachel. At first, I thought it was just a friendly chat to see how I was, but after a couple of minutes on the phone it became obvious that she wanted to update my story.

She had heard I'd trained to become a private investigator since the murder. Was that right? Did I have any theories as to who had murdered my husband? Had I trained to be a private investigator so I could catch the murderers?

"Look," I explained, "I'm leaving that with the police. If I get any ideas or find any evidence in my husband's possessions, I'll be sharing everything with them. I'm not, absolutely *not*, investigating crimes like that. I'll be investigating things that the police wouldn't normally handle."

I got the feeling she wasn't happy with that, and wanted to know where I would be operating from. When I let it slip that I would be leaving Brevelstone, she seemed to be losing interest.

"Well, I wish you well," she said, clearly disappointed. "I hope you don't mind if I run a short item with a few of your quotes."

"I haven't given you any quotes," I told her, trying to get rid of the woman. "Just talking about it is reviving too many memories. Sorry. Bye."

I didn't expect to read something on the front page a few days before I left for Button Up. *Local heartbroken woman turns Private Detective to capture husband's murderers. Janika Jones, wife of Sam Jones who was murdered at Mill Bridge six months ago, is still hunting for her husband's killers. "I will hand everything to the police," she promised me. "But I'm not going to rest until justice is done."*

Did I really say all that? Well, it's true, even though I'm sure I didn't express it in those words. I'm not going to make a complaint. I learnt on my course that it doesn't do to upset the press. Perhaps some good will come from it. Perhaps the woman who made the phone call was too scared to come forward at the time, maybe because she recognised somebody who was there. Maybe she'll come forward now so the police can identify the murderers. There had to be more than one in order to murder Sam. I can only hope there's a breakthrough.

This is my first night on my own since the night Sam died, because Jezza and Rachel insisted I immediately moved in with them. I'm lying on the comfy new bed with the firm mattress above Button Up, listening for the slightest sound, of which there are several. It seems the building creaks a lot at night. At least, I'm hoping that's what it is.

Abi has organised the whole apartment to be fitted with a sophisticated alarm with a digital keypad, to my specification – at my expense. The door at the top of the stairs is substantial, and the locksmith will shortly be fitting a metal bar across the inside, like the ones I've seen in some continental hotels for extra security at night.

Unless there are recording devices hardwired to a recording medium such as a memory card, the whole place is bug free. Exactly as I expected. I'm not worried about my personal safety. Okay, yes I am, but my main concern should be that clients' records on my premises are absolutely secure. So, a double benefit. Two birds killed with one stone. Stop thinking like that, Janika!

I feel a bit stupid for taking all these precautions. There's one safety precaution that seems a bit unnecessary, but I've purchased a rope ladder that will let me down from the living room window to the small parking area where Melanie and I have come to a satisfactory arrangement that allows us to park both our cars at the same time, but still give access to the waste skips.

The rope ladder is officially for use as a fire escape, of course. Actually, there's no rope involved. It has thin wires and aluminium rungs, so it rolls up neatly just below the window. Even I couldn't admit to myself that I might have reason to get out of here fast if someone was trying to break the door down. I know Abi didn't believe me about it being a fire escape, but I've got one all the same – on health and safety grounds. It's always good to remain safe.

I've bought an LED bedside light, and I'm hoping I can get to sleep with it on, set to low power. I'm not too keen on total darkness. I wondered if I'd picked up a tail shortly after leaving Brevelstone in my Nissan Micra. If I did, I lost it halfway here, although they could have been a second tail who took over to allay my suspicions. Quiet, girl, no one's interested in you anymore. You can relax.

But I can't relax. I know there's no tracker on my little car. My bug detector would have found it, no trouble. Yes, I really did check. I must be getting paranoid.

"Janika," I say aloud to myself, "there's only one thing that's worrying you, and that's whether you'll get work. All these other stupid imaginations are just that – stupid imaginations caused by low self-esteem about your ability to become a successful private detective." Note to self: be sure to take on easy jobs to start with.

The forensic investigation team didn't find any more bugs in Jezza and Rachel's house, which makes me feel proud of my first successful bug sweep that wasn't part of my course. They concluded that although the bugs were wired to the mains and therefore permanently active, there was no sign nearby that anybody had been tuning into them recently.

That confirms my suspicions that the bugs were placed as soon as the gang knew Sam and I were being evicted and moving there. So I can relax. The gang, whoever they are, are not interested in me at all. Just in Sam. And if Sam left any incriminating documents or notebooks behind, he certainly didn't leave them with me.

So I'm safe, unless they think I have evidence that will help convict them.

Well, I know there's nothing on the laptop. The police would have gone through every single file when they took it. And surely my phone is safe. Sam's phone never turned up, so I'm guessing the gang who murdered him took it in case there were things on there that would identify them.

Well, if somebody wants to find me, it's not going to be difficult. By setting myself up in business and advertising my name, I'm drawing attention to myself. Anyway, nothing special seems to have happened since Sam died. I've not come across anything that points the finger at Mr Big, to use an old-fashioned expression.

I've brought some personal belongings with me, including several books. Some of them are crime novels, which I started reading as soon as I decided to become a private investigator, hoping to pick up tips. There are some more serious books of help for private detectives, plus a few police handbooks that belonged to Sam, but I don't think any of them are going to make the right impression on my clients if they believe I need to keep referring to them – which I will do anyway, but not while they're watching. I gather Mr Jennings kept some accountancy books on top of the filing cabinet, but I've put all my books on a shelf in the living room-cum-bedroom.

I let Abi decide on the colour scheme and curtains, and she's done well. The smell of fresh paint reinforces the fact that I'm starting my life anew. I arrived here shortly before lunch, and ate down below in Button Up. I'm going to eat there regularly, because it would be rude not to. Anyway, I can't believe I'm going to find anywhere as good and friendly as the coffee shop. The staff seem to get on so well together.

I have to arrange to drop my Micra off at the garage where Abi's friend Rupert Forrester works. Because Jezza pointed out just how suitable the car would be for my work, I'm not going to bother with a quote. I want the dented door fixed, and anything that is potentially unreliable sorted. The garage is the other side of town, but Abi assures me Rupert will drop me back when I get round to making an appointment.

Abi knows of a sign maker in town, and I've ordered a suitable sign for the window that faces the street. Not the window with the new blind, but the one where Mr Jennings advertised his accountancy business. I'm also getting a small sign to go on the door to the street, so people know they've found the right place and don't go into the coffee shop by mistake.

Abi and I tested the original intercom, and it seems to work satisfactorily. It has a camera in it, connected to a small monitor on my desk. It's not exactly high-tech, but I'm not looking for things to spend my money on at this stage, although I do want to appear fully professional.

The sign maker has promised delivery in the morning. The locksmith is also coming in the morning to fit special security locks. As I explained to Abi, you never know who Mr Jennings gave keys to. And the locksmith is the one who will make the substantial door at the top of the stairs secure against forced intrusion by fitting the steel bar on the inside.

So everything kicks off in the morning. Maybe the new sign will bring in my first client, but I have to admit that's extremely unlikely. I need to visit the local newspaper office to see if they will give me an interview. That should get my name known. There's a digital LED clock on the shelf that says 2:33. I know it's right. I set it up myself with the time on my phone. It hardly seems worth going to sleep.

Chapter 11

I didn't realise Button Up would open so early. At seven o'clock I was woken by the sound of dragging chairs and tables, and a loud screeching from what is probably the coffee machine. But I can't complain. It's a cosy sound, even though it is a bit on the early side for me. I'll have to get into the habit of going to bed early to be sure of getting a good night's sleep.

Before eight, I'm sitting at the small table in the corner where Pete directs me. There are only two other people seated, and a small queue of men and women at the service counter with their own cups. I realise they are not intending to sit down, but taking coffee to work. They also seem to find the assorted pastries irresistible.

Well, if I'm going to make this a regular habit, I'll have to try one of them. Abi is here, but I get the impression she hasn't been here long. Poor Pete, having to cope on his own. I wonder where Melanie is.

The smell and the taste of Button Up coffee and the warm croissant with butter and raspberry jam slowly bring me back to life. I know I got very little sleep last night, but I'm not going to let that slow me down. The large clock shaped like a coffee cup above the service counter says five past eight. The sign for the upstairs window will be delivered at ten, and the locksmith is coming at the same time.

The print shop will open on the dot of nine – so Abi assures me. I need to take my memory stick with my carefully laid out flyer and business card master for professional printing. I've had too many pieces of junk mail through the door, badly composed and printed, to know that's not the way to go. Yes, I could print everything myself on my new inkjet, but I want something better. Not flash, just professional.

Of course, I could have sorted all this a few days ago, but the enormity of what I'm taking on really zapped my energy, and Rachel told me to take it easy. So the flyers and business cards were put on the backburner until I was sure of the premises and the name of my detective agency. I almost had to drag myself to town in my Micra last week to sort out the sign. I didn't come near here. I wanted to let Abi and her builder sort out the apartment without me poking my nose in.

I check the time on my phone, just in case the clock above the service counter is wrong. No, it's spot on. Time for another cappuccino. No, I'll make it a flat white this time. And perhaps another croissant. They are truly amazing. I tell myself this is not going to be a habit, but a treat, because this is my first day in business. But I don't really believe what I'm telling myself.

I'm staring at my phone. I've been using it for the last six months without any problem, since DI Dickinson took it away to check. I can't believe there's any sort of tracking device on there, and I'm no expert at finding spyware and trackers on phones and computers. I realise that as a matter of urgency I need to do two things. Abi comes across with my flat white and second croissant, and I ask if there's a good phone shop anywhere close. The sort of independent shop that fixes phones on the premises, and doesn't just sell them.

She says there's one in the next street, run by a young man who does all the work himself. It won't be open until nine o'clock. "Is there a problem?"

I smile. "I just need to get it cleaned." That's the truth. I *am* getting it cleaned – electronically. I also need to get an unregistered phone for emergencies. In one of the American novels I read it was called a burner phone, but its name isn't important. The phone shop guy will know what I mean.

I look at the clock again. Eight thirty. The time has gone on. I need to sort out a few things in my new office, and then visit the print shop and the phone shop, and be back here well before ten when the sign maker and locksmith come. They might even be early. I decide the print shop is the more important destination.

The man in the print shop looks about my age. He plugs my USB drive into the shop computer, and murmurs his approval at the image of the flyer that appears. I'm quite good at layout, and the wording and the clipart look professional. It was difficult to find suitable clipart. I didn't want cute pictures of Sherlock Holmes holding a large magnifying glass – of which there seemed to be hundreds. So instead, I settled for two fingerprints cut out in the shape of the letter J. I didn't want an ordinary fingerprint in case it looked as though someone with a grubby hand had already been holding the flyer, so I've chosen black and gold for everything. Of course, I'm now having grave doubts about black and gold, in case the gold comes out a yucky sort of yellow, but I might as well go for it. By coming here I've passed the point of no return.

My business cards are of a similar design. The quote isn't exactly a killer, so I can always come back for something different if I don't like them.

The man looks thoughtful. "Private detective? I didn't know we had one in town. I know Button Up. I use it myself sometimes, getting coffee on my way to work. What sort of jobs do you take on?"

I'm not sure if he's just making polite conversation, or if he has a possible assignment in mind. My first real job!

"Are you expensive?"

I assume he's asking about my fees, not anything personal. After all, he's wearing a wedding ring. I don't know if running a print shop is lucrative, but the young man doesn't look especially wealthy. "Do you have something in mind?"

"It's my little girl," he says. "My wife Daisy will be here soon. This is our print shop business. We can't very well bring little Katie to work, except in emergencies. So we get my Nan to look after Katie in the daytime."

It's my job as a detective to gather all the facts, not jump to conclusions with insufficient evidence. Even so, I think the man is about to tell me there's some sort of problem with his grandmother – and it's not medical.

"Go on," I say.

He's looking embarrassed. "I've heard you can hide a secret camera inside a clock or ornament, can't you?"

If I *have* to jump to a conclusion, I know where this is going. "You think there's a problem at home when you and your wife aren't there?"

He nods. "Since my Nan has been coming in, Katie seems to have been falling rather a lot. I don't like to say it, but I think you'll guess what we suspect. Katie is three years old, and quite steady on her feet. Every morning when my Nan comes in, Katie starts crying and hiding behind the curtains. Do you know where I can buy something with a camera hidden inside it?"

I feel so, so sorry. I desperately want to help, and I have the perfect clock I can lend him. Something pings in my head. I've just seen a brilliant way to advertise my services, without it costing me.

"In the circumstances, I'm happy to help. And it won't cost you a penny. I have exactly the clock you need in my office."

Actually, I have two such clocks. One of them is on the office wall recording everything that happens. It's for my own security, in case a client turns violent. What client?

"I can comc round this evening and set everything up. I take it you have wi-fi."

The man tells me he's called Tom Macdonald, and he nods. Yes, he has wi-fi. How will that help?

I'm about to explain, when Tom's wife Daisy arrives. I wait for Daisy to get behind the counter before I say anything more. I'm wondering what Daisy will think of

Tom's plan to spy on his grandmother.

Tom shows Daisy my artwork that's still on the monitor, and they have a confidential discussion. Daisy is looking back at me and she's smiling. It seems she and Tom are on the same page. "How much will all this camera equipment cost to set up?"

I return the smile. "I'm happy to do it for free. I can come round and set it up this evening, if that's okay. There's just one condition."

Tom and Daisy look at each other.

"There's just one condition," I repeat. "In return, I would like you to put a few flyers and my business cards on the counter."

Judging by their smiles, it looks as though we're getting a deal that suits both of us. I'll only be lending them the clock for a few days, and since I already have one, it isn't going to cost me anything. "But I insist I pay for the printing."

I'm outside the print shop now. "Well," I say aloud, "that certainly went well. Even if only one person comes to give me work because of the flyers on the counter, it will be sufficient reward. I wonder if Abi and Melanie will let me leave some on the counter at Button Up. Maybe even at the phone shop, which is where I have to go now."

I need to hurry to the phone shop. I have to be back in plenty of time to receive the sign and let the locksmith get to work.

Chapter 12

As I step into the small, untidy shop, arrayed with a range of phones both new and used, I'm wishing I'd waited until I had some business cards. I'm about to ask the young guy behind the counter if he will check my phone over for any possible nasties. It would look much more impressive if I had one of my cards.

He doesn't laugh when I explain I'm a private investigator. Perhaps he even believes me. I tell him I want my phone serviced, and while he's at it, would he just check that there is no spyware, including a tracker. I manage to force an embarrassed smile as I ask.

To my surprise, he's taking the request seriously. Perhaps he likes playing at spies, and this is his first chance to get involved.

"How long will it take?" I ask. "I really don't want to be without a phone for long." And now I have to present a convincing case for needing a burner phone, which hopefully he'll let me have without too much fuss. "Tell you what, I could do with a cheap backup phone. Something I can just top up at the supermarket or the cashpoint. Because of my sensitive work, I don't always want my phone calls to be traced back to me." I put on a winning smile. "Nothing illegal, but I just need to be careful sometimes. Private investigation work can be dangerous."

That's a lie. Well, it's not really a lie if I'm talking

about private investigation work in general. It's just that mine is unlikely to be dangerous, but of course it's always possible. That makes me feel better. Or perhaps worse.

Business seems to be quiet, and I get his full attention. He suggests I don't buy a cheap phone, but a refurbished good quality one for the same price. That sounds great, and within ten minutes I'm on my way back to Button Up with a classy phone with an unregistered pay-as-you-go SIM card preloaded with twenty pounds. I'm hoping no one needs to contact me urgently, as obviously no one will be able to phone me on this. Even I can't remember the number yet, but I have it written down. Anyway, he's promised my regular phone by three o'clock this afternoon, and I guess that's not going to present me with any problems.

It's not yet ten o'clock, and I can see Button Up at the end of the road. There's no one hanging around outside, so I'm probably back in time. I go in and ask Abi if anyone has been looking for me. No one has. But just at that moment I see a large van arrive outside with sign writing all over it.

I hurry out and open the street door to my apartment. As I open it, I just love the refurbished stairs and walls. Abi and her builder certainly did a good job – apparently with some help from Abi's husband and friends. I'm surprised Mr Jennings worked from here as it was. I'm sure an untidy entrance area isn't conducive to instilling confidence in clients.

The middle-aged man who is delivering my sign insists on taking it up to the office. It seems that men, both old and young, want to go out of their way to help me. It can't be because of my looks, so perhaps I come over as a helpless female. Well, whatever the reason, I'm glad I have that effect.

The man unwraps the sign and I stand back to look at it. It's amazing. When I'd called at the shop, the woman in the office had brought up a few possibilities on the computer, and this was the design and colour scheme I'd chosen. But to see it actually full-size, here in my office, is wonderful.

"Where's it going?" the man asks.

"In the window," I say. "My friends are going to fix it up there for me, so you can just leave it against the wall for now. You have the small one for the front door?"

I want to show the small one to Abi. Hopefully she or one of her friends will be able to screw it for me onto the street door. Memo to self: get some tools, you never know when they'll come in handy.

Just as the man drives off, another van arrives. It's like a pitstop. This van has the name of my locksmith on it. People in this small town are certainly reliable, I'll say that for them. I'm gasping for another fix of coffee after what has already been a busy morning, but I have to stay out of Button Up for the moment. I can leave the locksmith to get on with things, but first I need to check that he's brought the two high security locks I chose when he called to give the quote. And, of course, the strong steel bar to go inside the door at the top of the stairs.

There are two locks. A multi-lever deadlock with three hardened circular bolts to resist saws and angle grinders, and an anti-snap, anti-pick, anti-drill and anti-bump lock, together with a double cylinder latch that locks itself automatically on both sides when the door closes – according to the technical specification he showed me. The door already has a closing spring on it, and I tell him I want to be sure it really will latch by itself.

All seems well with the locks he's had to order specially for this job, and I explain that the high security alarm – and I'm emphasising the high security part – is not set, and under no circumstances is he to let anyone upstairs. If anyone comes looking for me, I'm in Button Up.

As I turn to leave, a sudden thought occurs to me. I remember being advised about security on my course. If you lock yourself accidentally out of your house, how would you get in? And the answer is – the way the housebreaker would choose! "So if you had to get in here without keys," I ask him, "how would you do it?"

I get the feeling the man just wants me to leave him alone so he can get on with the job. He shrugs. "Dynamite?"

I nod. "Yeah, that would do it."

As I enter Button Up, I can see that the small table at the far end is unoccupied. There already seems to be something special about sitting there. Of course, it means I can keep an eye on the whole coffee shop, but I can't really see the importance of that. I'm not here to spy on the customers!

Oh, I can see a Reserved sign on the table. That's a shame. Someone catches me by the arm and before I can steady myself, I'm being steered towards the table. It's Abi.

"I always reserve it for Danny," she explains. "He sits here to have his lunch, but you're welcome to sit here now." She motions to me to sit down, but leaves the Reserved sign there. So at least I won't be getting any unwelcome customers wanting to share the table. I really need to sit quietly and think.

Is Tom at the print shop's grandmother really harming Katie? Perhaps the little girl just keeps bumping into things. Anyway, if the video from the spy clock shows the grandmother giving the most loving attention to the little girl, while Katie keeps crashing into the furniture, at least the reason for the bruises will be obvious, and the parents can relax. There might be a medical problem, and not one of abuse.

As soon as I can get upstairs, I need to make sure the spy clock is ready to go. I know people put them in care homes to keep an eye on a vulnerable relative, and that presents a difficulty. With the built-in battery, although the clock keeps running, the recording will only last for a few hours.

The clock ideally needs connecting to the mains electricity, but in a care home every item with a plug needs to be safety tested. I roll my eyes. The electrician is, of course, almost certain to wonder why a simple electric wall clock needs mains electricity. Unless he or she can be tipped off in advance and is sympathetic to the reason for the clock being there in the first place, there can be problems.

I don't need to give my order. Without me saying a word, Abi brings me my cappuccino. I'm a devotee of the frothy top as well as the flavour. The apple Danish is a surprise, but Abi smiles and puts a finger to her lips. "A little treat on the house."

I very nearly say, "A moment on the lips and a lifetime on the hips," but that might not be a tactful thing to say to Abi who has been so kind to me!

From the word go, I've insisted on paying for my own coffee. I like to think of the staff as friends, and indeed they are, but I want to keep the relationship on a professional footing. I'm a tenant, not a guest.

I'm just giving Abi the number of my burner phone and explaining the reason for having it, when I jump. Someone is just inside the coffee shop, calling my name. It's a man. It's not the locksmith. I can see his van outside, and I'm sure he'll call to see me to check the locks before he leaves. The man is standing with the light behind him, but I recognise him immediately. I jump to my feet as he comes across to the table.

"Detective Inspector Dickinson," I say. "Have you come with any special news?" Oh, I hope he has. Catching the murderers won't bring Sam back to life, but I'll feel much safer when they're all locked away.

He points to the empty chair. "May I?"

"Of course. Would you like a coffee? Are you on your own?" I'm half expecting to see Courtney Jacobs. I'm assuming the detective inspector is here on duty and hasn't just come for the coffee and my company.

"It's only a courtesy call," he explains. "As Sam's

team leader, I feel a certain responsibility for you."

There's a long pause, and then he says, "I wish you hadn't gone to the press. It puts us in an embarrassing light when people think an amateur detective is trying to solve the case."

"A professional private investigator," I say, "but the woman got it all wrong. I assured her that if I have any evidence, I'll turn it straight over to the police. She didn't bother to quote where I told her my job wouldn't be fighting crime. I'm sorry if anyone took it the wrong way."

I think the detective inspector believes me, but he looks concerned. "I want you to promise me again, Janika, that under no circumstances will you investigate your husband's murder. Promise? Seriously promise this time? I like you, Janika, and I don't want you getting hurt." And he reaches across and touches my hand. I withdraw it slowly, so as not to appear rude. I wish he hadn't done that.

He merely shrugs and points to the ceiling. Presumably he's indicating my apartment. "How are you settling in, Janika? Plenty of work?"

Spying on an elderly relative for the MacDonalds doesn't exactly sound glamorous, so I merely tell him it's early days, but there is already some definite interest.

Once again he points to the ceiling. "Courtney has told me about your office. Is it all right if I have a look?"

I'm just about to say that's fine, when I suddenly wonder exactly what the man's motives are. Is he hitting on me? Courtney said his wife and kids have recently left him. Is he lonely enough to come all the way here from Brevelstone to try and pick me up? Perhaps talking about the newspaper report was a convenient cover story. This isn't looking good.

I put on a pretence of a smile. The man is probably nearly twenty years older than me. His lack of hair isn't a problem. Sam might have gone completely bald by that age, if he'd lived. But the straggly moustache would have to go. Not that I'm even thinking about any sort of relationship with DI Dickinson. My mind is behaving most oddly.

"Of course you can have a look round," I say. "But have a coffee first. And the restroom is that way." I'm certainly not having him poking around in my living quarters. Just the office.

Before he can raise a finger for service, because he's being watched with great interest by Abi, Melanie and Pete, I jump to my feet and tell him I'll get the coffee for him.

He wants a large latte, and as I walk across to the service counter I give the order loudly. Then when I'm really close, I whisper to Abi, "He wants to look round upstairs. Please, please come with me."

Abi starts to laugh. "Don't you trust him? You can always trust a policeman. That's what my mother told me."

"Something doesn't feel right," I say with a frown, hoping the Happy Button will take me seriously.

"What excuse shall I give?"

I give a brief smile. "I know you'll think of something. Just don't let me down."

Chapter 13

I turn to go back to the table, and it's empty. Now where's the man gone? Two minutes later I hear the flush going in the unisex toilet followed by the noise of the hand dryer. Then Detective Inspector Dickinson appears. I hope he didn't overhear what I was saying to Abi when he must have gone past us just now.

The locksmith calls from the doorway to say he needs me. I tell DI Dickinson that his coffee is on the way, and I'll be back. I think his name is Roger, but I'm not sure. I really need to find out, although if he really *is* keen on me, maybe it's best to keep things on a formal footing.

The locksmith says he's finished, and he hands me three sets of keys. I'm not going to let him go until I'm satisfied with his workmanship. I try out each of the locks in turn, several times from the outside, and then from the inside. He seems to have done the perfect job.

"These are the most secure locks I can get my hands on for this design of wooden door," the locksmith says. "They are drill proof and bump proof, but if someone is determined enough they'll cut their way in with drills and grinders. But if you're here at the time, you'll have plenty of warning to phone the police and get out through the back window." He shrugs. "And if they try in the middle of the day, when you're out, some suspicious neighbour is going to phone the police anyway. Just remember, no the door is proof against a determined professional."

That sounds fine to me, and one of the things we learnt on our course is that even the most secure vault in the world can be broken into given enough time. The main thing is to delay the intruder long enough to get help or escape. Ideally both.

The locksmith hasn't finished yet with his cheerful advice. "Don't forget, the latch you ordered locks itself automatically from both sides when the door closes. You'll need your key to get out, or you could be burnt to death if the place is on fire. This double cylinder latch is really intended for separate areas connected by a single door that only authorised people with a key can come backwards and forwards through. Remember, as soon as the door closes, it locks itself."

That all seems straightforward enough, but I feel an explanation is called for. "With the double cylinder latch bolt I can't leave here without my keys and lock myself out. And I always want to come down the stairs to welcome a client in at the door, and see them out the same way, so I'll always have the key with me. So it's just the metal bar on the inside of the door at the top of the staircase," I say.

"As long as you know where your keys are if you have to get out in a hurry," the locksmith says. "I'm serious."

I nod. "All taken care of. I have a fire escape at the back of the building, so there's no need to worry about me."

I don't think he looks especially worried anyway. I

think he just wants to put himself in the clear in case I get trapped in the front of the burning building and can't find the key. I've already decided what to do. There are three sets of keys I've ordered. One for me, a set for Abi for emergencies, and I'm going to slip the spare double cylinder latch key under the stair carpet on the third step up. It's not like putting a key under the doormat. Someone would already have to be inside the building to be able to search for it. In which case, they wouldn't need it anyway.

I remind the locksmith about the bar he's fitting to the door at the top of the stairs. That's good, because even if Abi can't get away, I'll have the locksmith there when the detective inspector has his self-invited look round the office.

"Already done," locksmith says with a smile. "You'd better check it, and then I'll be on my way. And here's the invoice. I have a card reader if you'd like to pay me now."

The man isn't missing a trick. I run up the stairs quickly and check the metal bar. It's exactly what I hoped for. So I have no reason to delay him. I have my debit card in the pocket of my jeans. It feels great to know that my cards are no longer maxed out, and I don't have to put on an elaborate display of pretending to wonder what's gone wrong at the bank.

By this time, Abi appears with DI Dickinson. "Is it all right if I come up with you?" Abi asks. "I'd like to see what the locksmith has done on the door at the top of the stairs."

Crafty Abi. There, I knew she would come up with a

good excuse. "Yes, come on. You can lead the way."

I want DI Dickinson to go next. I always feel uncomfortable with a man following me closely up the stairs with his eyes at butt level, even though I don't have a figure to lust after. But he insists on taking up the rear. Not a good choice of word.

We reach the top without me experiencing any groping hands, and I feel stupid. The detective might be missing his family, or perhaps he was glad to see them go. Either way, he isn't interested in me. This has to be nothing more than a social visit by someone who knew Sam and wants to make sure I'm surviving okay.

Abi spots the large sign for the window leaning against the front wall. She lets out a noise that implies full approval, and DI Dickinson smiles. "Very professional," he says. "I hope you really do make a go of it, Janika."

I'm wishing I knew what his first name is. I can't keep referring to him as Detective Inspector. He glances around the office and pats the top of the desk. "Very nice. Very nice indeed."

He smiles as he points to the clock on the wall. "Is that what I think it is?"

Abi frowns. "It's a clock," she says, stating the obvious.

Both the detective and I laugh. "It's a camera as well," I explain. "You can *just* see the tiny camera lens in the figure ten if you look really closely. It's what's called a pinhole camera, because the lens is no bigger than the head of a pin."

"Oh," Abi says, "is it working now?" And she runs her hands through her long blonde hair, and smoothes down her black and cream striped Button Up jacket.

"Twenty-four seven," I say, amused by her reaction. "Don't worry, Abi, I won't be doing a public screening of this visit on YouTube."

DI Dickinson sits in the impressive swivel office chair behind the impressive mahogany desk. "You deserve to do well, Janika," he says. "Sam would be proud of you if he could see you now."

"Perhaps he can," I say. "He said he was a Christian." There, that should kill any ideas of romance in the detective's balding head.

I notice Abi almost jump. "I didn't know," she says. "What about you, Janika? Do you go to church?"

This is all getting a bit personal. I pull a face. "Not really," I say, leaving the whole thing rather vague. Everybody should be entitled to their own belief, and not get quizzed about it by religious do-gooders.

From the hurt look on Abi's face I feel sorry for being so snappy. Especially after she's been good enough to come up to play gooseberry with me and DI Dickinson. I'll have to make it up to her later.

It's time to come clean. "I'm sorry," I say to the detective nspector, "but I don't remember your first name."

I put my hand to my mouth metaphorically, hoping it didn't sound as though I was expressing a personal interest.

He smiles as he says, "You must call me Roger."

Roger – I'm not sure I'm going to get used to referring to the man informally yet – spends a little time looking around the office, but as he goes to open the door to the living quarters, Abi very diplomatically takes him by the arm. "That's all private," she says with a laugh. "Come downstairs, and have another coffee and something to eat."

Abi is amazing. I'll never, ever hold anything against her. She seems to have a remarkable ability to read situations in advance. I don't think that's anything you could learn on a residential PI course. I just hope it's something that's also built into me. I'm certainly going to need it in my work as a private investigator.

I'm wondering how Tom MacDonald's grandmother is going to react when she discovers she's been secretly recorded on video. Of course, unless he's stupid, Tom isn't going to tell her if there's no sign of abuse, and the grandmother is genuinely taking great care of her granddaughter. Perhaps little Katie needs to see a doctor about why she bruises so easily. So, either way, something good is bound to happen from me taking on the case. My first *professional* case. It's so simple that it definitely can't go wrong.

I follow behind Roger and Abi as we leave, making sure they go in front so I can lock the door at the top of the stairs. It's not a high security lock, but even if someone manages to get through the outside door, the alarm will instantly trip, and they'll be trapped on the stairs.

The window at the back, where I have the rolled up ladder for the fire escape, is a substantial white uPVC construction with a locking handle. No one can get in that way. And if anyone tries, there's now a vibration sensor on the glass, connected to the main alarm.

Roger pauses and examines the stairway sensors and the digital control box. "It all looks good to me," he says, turning back and giving me a smile. "With all these precautions, there's one thing you can be sure about, Janika. You're going to be safe here."

I pass him the new key to the double cylinder lock. "You're going to need this to get out. That latch locks itself when the door closes."

Chapter 14

I'm feeling lost without my usual phone. Not that anyone is going to be contacting me about a possible investigation. Those flyers aren't out yet, and although Pete has helped me place my large sign with my mobile number in the window, it's unlikely anyone will phone today.

I'm really regretting not getting the flyers and business cards organised earlier, but at least something good has come out of it. The MacDonalds are going to display my flyers and business cards on the counter, and they gave me my first commission. I didn't expect to be snooping on a grandmother, but it's work, even though I'm not being paid. Well, I thought all along that I might need to get involved in pro bono work to get my name known.

Just after two o'clock my spare phone rings. That's strange, because nobody knows the number yet, apart from Abi. I answer it cautiously. "Hello?"

Much to the surprise of the man on the other end, I burst out laughing when he explains who it is. How stupid can I be! It's the phone shop guy. He actually noted the number of the SIM card when he fitted it in my spare phone.

He tells me my phone is now clean.

"I'll be with you immediately. ... What message?"

In my excitement I wasn't really listening. "The print shop? Thanks. See you soon."

Things are getting better and better. Apparently Tom at the print shop has sent a text to say that my printing is ready to collect, and phone shop guy spotted it on the screen just after he'd finished putting everything back together. Note to self: get him to confirm that there are definitely no secret apps on there.

I'm at the print shop now, and Tom and Daisy are looking pleased with themselves as they hand me two packages. Taped on the top of each one is a sample of what's inside. Both the flyers and the business cards look absolutely amazing. The quality feels outstanding as I run my finger over them. The gold really looks like gold, against a glossy black background. Expensive. No wonder the MacDonalds are grinning.

I hope they stick with the quote they gave me when I dropped the job off. I'm getting my debit card out of my bag to pay, just hoping that there hasn't been a rush charge. I mean, they look really, really classy. I wasn't expecting them until tomorrow.

They tell me to put my card away, but I remind them that I said I was going to pay for them, but not charge them for lending them the spy clock – on the condition that they place some flyers and business cards on the counter.

Still grinning, Tom points to a little cardboard stand that contains a batch of my flyers and business cards. Great, but they're not exactly prominent or I would have spotted them to begin with.

"We can't possibly charge you," Daisy says. "We really appreciate the offer of the clock. You can come around any time after six. Tom's Nan will have gone by then. It won't take long, will it?"

I'm only half listening. I don't have the cheek to ask them to move the small display stand to somewhere a bit more prominent, but both Tom and Daisy turn their backs for a moment and I surreptitiously slide the display forward, and stand there innocently while I make a note of their address.

Now to the phone shop with my freshly printed flyers. I'm wondering if phone shop guy will be amenable to leaving some on the counter. I'm certainly going to give it a go. I'm not the timid creature I was at school. Meeting Abi again has brought back all sorts of memories of that time, plus the horrific relationship with Bruno Kamiński in Poland. No wonder I came back to England.

Phone shop guy is smiling. He says he's checked my phone and he's found one suspicious app on there, but it seems he has no idea what it did. It wasn't a tracking device, but it was definitely some sort of spyware. But he's deleted it anyway, and given it a full virus and malware check of his own.

I have to admit I can't share his smile. As a private investigator my phone has to be cleaner than clean. I'm wondering when the spyware got on there. Probably when I was doing a Google search and clicked on a dodgy site. I've always believed my antivirus app would sort out that type of thing.

Anyway, I thank him profusely, and am more than happy with the cost. He's given my phone a physical as well as an electronic clean.

I take a deep breath. Come on, girl, you're no longer a mouse. "I'm wondering if you would be good enough to put a few of these flyers on the counter. Or perhaps some of my business cards. In return, I'll recommend you to anyone who has a phone problem. How's that?" I'm sounding much more confident than I feel. I've learnt to do that.

Phone shop guy looks at the flyers and points to his very cluttered counter. "Leave a few business cards. Call in occasionally, and you can leave some more if I run out."

I think he rather fancies me. Well, it's a one-way fancy, but I smile. "Yes, great idea. And you know how to phone me if you run out extra quickly."

I'm glad to get out of the shop, although I'm relieved to have my phone checked and cleaned. I could have bought a new one, but this one is an old friend. So now I have to go back to my new office and wait for the phone to ring with requests for my services. In the meantime, I really fancy one of Button Up's jam doughnuts. Liam won't be back from school yet, so there's a good chance there'll be at least one left.

<><><><>

I've only just sat down for my coffee and jam doughnut when my phone rings. Unfortunately, it isn't a potential client. It's my mother, phoning from Poland to check up on me.

I've not seen my parents since Sam's funeral, and we don't have much contact. My mother can't forgive me for leaving Bruno, and refused to believe just what a control freak and bully he was. Whenever he hit me, he always did it below the waist where it wouldn't show.

Bruno is the son of one of my father's Polish friends, and my parents thought it was going to be a marriage made in heaven. Fortunately, the marriage never took place. Sometimes I feel sad, like I do now, and wonder what our child would look like if he had been born. It was six serious blows to the stomach that caused the miscarriage. Only five months old, but still a baby boy. My child.

I was too scared to tell the hospital what had happened, and my mother wouldn't believe that the injury had been responsible. "You're young," she told me. "Miscarriages happen. Plenty of time for you and Bruno to have another."

That's when I fled to England, where I met Sam. Sam was the most gentle, loving man I could ever hope to meet. I've heard that physically and emotionally abused women can go into a series of similar relationships, but fortunately not me.

Anyway, my mother says she and Dad are coming over, and they want to make sure I'm living in a nice place. Well, it *is* nice, but they're probably expecting something much more luxurious, and not just a bedsit attached to an upstairs office.

"No, *Matka*," – that's Polish for mother – "there isn't room for you both to stay with me. ... I'll definitely find you a nice hotel. ... No, there's only one bed."

Eventually the phone call finishes, and I really don't fancy my coffee. It's gone cold, and the jam doughnut looks too big a mouthful to cope with, the way I'm feeling. I'm wondering why my mother, my *matka*, is having this effect on me. I'm thirty-three and have a life of my own, away from my controlling parents. What did she mean, do I have a steady boyfriend now? How dare she! No one can replace my Sam.

There's a folded newspaper on the table. Perhaps there will be something there that will take my mind off my parental problems. It's folded back at a crossword. I look closely and it seems to be a cryptic one. I remember Abi saying she likes to do cryptic crosswords. Perhaps this is one of hers. Well, it's not finished yet. I think I'll surprise her and fill in a couple of clues. Assuming I can.

Four down. More of a cryptic clue than an anagram. It has to start with the letters F A. Okay, it's FAMILY. I wonder if Abi will mind if I fill it in. My pen is in my bag. No, Family won't fit. The last letter has to be an R.

Abi comes across and is surprised to see my coffee has not been drunk. "Is there a problem?"

I feel like bursting into tears and confiding in her

about the phone call I've just received, but I force a smile. "Sorry, my mother rang and I got rather distracted." I'm hoping Abi won't ask what caused the distraction.

Abi offers to get me a fresh coffee, and she spots the pen in my hand and the folded newspaper. "See if you can get four down," she says. "I'm completely stuck on that one."

"Me too."

While Abi goes to get my fresh coffee, I study the crossword again. And then I laugh. Six across is Quicker, not Quickly. So everything fits.

Pete follows Abi across as she brings me my coffee. Pete points to the newspaper. "Are you good at that sort of thing, Janika?"

I shrug. "Sometimes."

Pete laughs. "We pull Abi's leg about her crosswords. If she doesn't know one of the answers, she looks it up on the internet."

I can see Abi turning red. "Not true, Pete. Yes, if I'm stuck I try to find the answers online, but only so I can see how the clue works. So I can learn for next time. If I get help with a crossword, I never claim to have completed it by myself." She turns to me. "Honest."

"But she leaves the folded paper on one of the tables for the customers to see," Pete whispers, loudly enough for Abi to hear.

"Pete, I think the toilet needs cleaning," Abi says, winking at me. "And then you can tidy the stockroom."

Pete is obviously used to this putdown, and he takes no notice. Melanie and a rather self-conscious looking ginger haired boy appear from round the back. Liam has something wrapped in white tissue paper.

"Sherlock Holmes," he says, as I start to unwrap the tissue paper. "You said you liked him."

"Liam," I say, "it's wonderful. Sherlock Holmes is my hero. Every time I get out my keys I'll remember him. And I'll remember you, too."

In my hand I'm holding a coloured plastic key ring in the shape of the famous detective. It makes me smile to see the comic representation of Sherlock Holmes, but it really is a great present. Liam has backed away. Perhaps he thinks I'm going to give him a kiss. So I thank him again, and get out the key fob to my Nissan Micra and attach it while he watches from a safe distance.

Given half a chance I would have kissed him. It's wonderful to be given such a moving pressie, especially by a small lad who is apparently so excited that I'm here. I know I'm a disappointment to my mother, but I hope I'm not going to be a disappointment to the boy.

Chapter 15

Tom and Daisy Macdonald's house is on the edge of Craidlea. It's an area I don't remember visiting when we lived here in a previous lifetime. If my parents had let me have a bicycle, as many other kids had at school, I would have explored around a bit. Compared to Brevelstone, the place is tiny, surrounded by countryside.

It's seven o'clock and I get a good welcome. Daisy shows me the room where Tom's Nan looks after Katie most of the day. The little girl is looking at me now, and she gives a shy smile. Daisy has introduced me to her as a good friend. Sensible, even if not true. Tom and Daisy are about my age, so perhaps it's some sort of subconscious wish on their part.

I don't want to intrude too much on family time, but it's important that both Tom and Daisy understand what's happening with the clock. It needs to be placed where the wide-angle lens will include as much of the room as possible. It also needs to be near a mains socket to keep the battery charged up, otherwise the recording only lasts for five or six hours. And that's usually a big problem.

Modern clocks run on a small battery, and don't have a long lead dangling from them. However, there's a bookcase with a table lamp on the top shelf. The lamp obviously plugs into something, and if I put the clock on there it will be more or less pointing in the right direction. Not perfect, but good enough.

Daisy is interested in checking where the lens is. I point out the small black dot in the figure one of the ten. It's so small and insignificant that she doesn't spot it for a moment. Now she's smiling.

"That's a big relief," she says, laughing. "Somehow I had a vision of a large glass camera lens staring out at us. Amazing. And this really works?"

I'm not offended. The world of spy cameras is obviously new to Daisy. It was a revolutionary design of lens that came out many years ago. The front part of it is really small, which means cameras can be concealed in almost anything. And since this camera records onto its own memory card, it is extremely difficult to discover with the more basic bug detectors. To discover a camera with the basic detector, it needs to transmit a radio frequency signal. So no one can snoop on this camera. Except they can, with the right equipment.

"I need your wi-fi code," I say.

Daisy says she wants to put Katie to bed, and leaves me with Tom.

I explain that with the wi-fi connection, he and Daisy will be able to monitor what's happening on their phone.

"I don't understand," Tom says. "We're already here. We can see what's going on."

I have to remember this sort of technology is something I've been trained to use. "You will be able to log into your wi-fi at work, and receive a live stream from the clock."

He looks surprised, but obviously believes me. "That's amazing, Janika, I didn't realise it would be so easy. That means if we see something happening that we don't like, one of us can go straight home. But is it also being recorded? I'm thinking that my Nan is going to deny everything."

Tom certainly seems convinced that something unpleasant is going on when he and Daisy are at work. I explain that the memory card will only record for about eight hours, without being replaced or downloaded. When the clock is connected to the mains electricity, it will keep recording whenever there is enough light, but the recording will start overwriting everything on there when the card is full.

Tom is so impressed with what I've set up for the family, that I'm sure he'll be singing my praises to every customer he gets. I just hope his Nan doesn't find out what we've done – if she turns out to be totally innocent.

Tom gives me the house wi-fi code, and I link it to the clock. I'm glad I've practised this a few times, because I want to look fully professional, not trying to read the tiny Chinese instruction booklet as I go. I ask Tom for his phone, and we connect the two. Fortunately, all is well.

Tom seems to be amazed by the picture he gets. He walks around the room, staring at his phone in his hand, and occasionally waving to the camera. He's like a small child with a new birthday present. Then he tells me to stand and wave, while he pops up to Katie's bedroom and shows the picture to Daisy.

"Don't forget," I say, "that camera is recording all the time. I can set it so it only records when it detects movement, but I'm sure you're interested in what might be happening off camera. Don't forget, it records sound as well. So you need to remember that. Anything you and Daisy get up to in the evening is going to be recorded."

Tom grins. "Duly noted, Janika. Anyway, we're not going to post this on Twitter, so it will be..." He pauses. "No one else can see these pictures on their *own* phone, can they?"

I assure him that only someone connected to his wi-fi is able to see the pictures, and his security code is a good one. The only reason I gave him the warning was in case someone got hold of the memory card and enjoyed themselves snooping on family life.

I promise Tom I'll call at the print shop in the morning and check his phone, to make sure there are no problems in getting a clear picture. All being well, he will be able to monitor what's happening at home. I'm guessing it will be frequently. Perhaps continually.

I realise this isn't the end of it. If there *is* some sort of physical abuse, I'll have to get Tom or Daisy to switch to clock off before the recording gets overwritten. Then either they or I can run the recording on one of our laptops in front of what will presumably be an extremely irate grandmother – on the assumption that she's guilty. Well, that's what a private investigator has to do. I have to distance myself from getting caught up in the emotions.

<><><><>

I'm back now in my apartment, and it's already dark outside. I didn't want to intrude too long on Tom and Daisy's hospitality. If a friendship develops, all well and good, but I'm feeling exhausted. I don't mind my parents coming, but I don't want my mother keeping on about finding a nice man. I wouldn't put it past her to bring Bruno. No, that's clearly not going to happen. I think eventually she started to believe me about the abuse.

I'm feeling snug and secure. There are two separate parts to the alarm system. One connected to the outer door and staircase, and one for the apartment. I've set the one for the outer door, but will only be able to set the alarm system in the apartment when I'm out. The slightest movement will trigger it.

I'm sitting in one of the small leather armchairs by the window. I've not put the blind down yet, and I don't intend to do it. I want people passing by to see me, and get the impression that I'm a workaholic. What no one can see is the eBook reader in my hand. I'm halfway through a cosy detective story. I've already guessed who the baddie is, but of course it won't be him. That's how these detective stories work.

I've read a few books where I could only guess who the murderer is by ruling out every possible candidate except the one it *can't* be. And of course that's the person it is. I'm not so keen on authors who write like that. I prefer it if there are clues I can use along the way and guess the culprit, even if I can't see how they are going to be caught. If I get it right, which I do occasionally, that makes me feel satisfied with my detecting skills.

I let out a long, loud yawn. So much has happened today. My phone is fixed, my flyers and business cards are printed, and I've carried out my first assignment as a professional private investigator. It's time for an early night.

Just as I get out of my chair, the doorbell rings.

Chapter 16

Well, I'm certainly not going to hurry down and open the door. That's what the intercom is for. For some reason I feel anxious as I hold down the Talk button. A grainy black-and-white picture of the road outside appears on the desk monitor, but no face. "Yes?"

No one answers.

"Yes?" I repeat.

Still no answer.

It's probably some silly teenagers passing by who thinks it's funny to ring the bell and keep walking. I must remember to switch off the intercom at night. There doesn't seem to be a switch, but I'm sure one can easily be arranged. Perhaps this happens often in the evening, and all through the night.

Apparently Mr Jennings had a hearing problem, so he probably wouldn't have known what was going on. Especially if he was in bed, with his hearing aids on the night stand. I wonder what Mr Jennings was like. Perhaps I'll be able to meet him sometime. I gather he's living in an old folks' apartment on the edge of town.

I feel a bit uneasy. Well, no one has managed to get through the front door. The green alarm light is showing above the door to the top of the stairs, indicating that the alarm system is live. Unless the locksmith has given keys to someone, there's no way even the most determined intruder can get through the front door without making a huge amount of noise. But, even *if* they have somehow managed it silently, they won't know the alarm code. The alarm company is completely separate to the locksmith. So unless there's a criminal gang consisting of locksmith and alarm company operating in town, I'm safe.

The office door to the stairs has the steel bar in place. I know I'm chicken, but I want to be a very safe chicken. I wait a few minutes, and there's no sound from below. Button Up closes on the dot of six, so it does feel a bit lonely here. Quite a bit of noise comes up from the coffee shop during the day, and I find that very comforting. It's the silence at night, like now, that isn't so good.

Being all on my own at night in an empty building, after staying with Jezza and Rachel for several months, is scary enough – without hearing lots of little noises. In the end, my nosiness, or inquisitiveness, gets the better of me. I feel an urge to unhook the steel bar and just peep down the stairs before going to bed. I'm a child again, looking under my bed for a bogeyman before I can climb in and go to sleep. How could there possibly be a bogeyman on the stairs? But I feel compelled to look.

With my phone in my hand, and 999 set on speed dial, I slide the steel bar back and open the door as silently as I can. I've left the staircase light on, because I'm not yet as laid-back as I should be. Well, this is a strange apartment in a strange town, and I really do feel a bit isolated. Most of all, I miss my Sam.

I look down the staircase. No one. But there's something on the mat just inside the front door. Why someone would ring the bell to let me know they put a note through the door, I have no idea, but it's safe for me to go down and retrieve it.

I'm holding a plain white envelope, and I open it. This can't be real. Why would someone send me this?

DO NOT TRY TO INVESTIGATE YOUR HUSBAND'S DEATH OR YOU WILL END UP THE SAME

"I've no intention of investigating it," I say aloud, as though the writer of the note can hear me. It's obviously been done on a computer and printed on an inkjet printer. I immediately drop the paper and envelope to the floor.

It's a joke, obviously. But it's not funny. How does anyone connected with Sam's murder even know I'm here? Well, of course word will have got round, but why would anyone come all this way to do something so stupid? Just reading it has probably caused me more hurt than the writer intended. Well, they're not going to get away with this.

I pop back upstairs and get some latex gloves from my forensic kit, and a plastic evidence bag. In the old days, especially in detective stories, the note would have been typewritten, and the detective would point out that the T was slightly crooked, or some other misplacement of one of the keys. All they had to do was test a few typewriters and, bingo, the guilty party was discovered.

Now, with computers and printers, that option has disappeared, although I did read somewhere that each printer has some microscopic anomaly. I don't have the technology to do it, but there may be fingerprints on the paper, and DNA on the envelope. But who's going to bother to check for it?

This is clearly some sort of stupid practical joke. I could show it to Courtney Jacobs, but she won't be able to get any support. It is not as though I've been physically attacked. And why would anyone think I'm investigating Sam's death. That's with Brevelstone's CID. Oh yes, that's what I allegedly said in that newspaper article. I know DI Dickinson doesn't seem to have been making much progress, but I'm certainly not going to interfere.

I'm trying to put a brave face on things, but this note has really scared me. We're talking murder here. My husband's murder. Perhaps I *will* contact Courtney in the morning. If the author of the note can be identified, they can at least be threatened with prosecution if they don't desist. The more I think about it, the more angry I feel, and the more determined I am to get revenge.

It looks like I'm heading for another night of broken sleep, I'm so worked up. I made a mistake in sitting by the window. What did I think, that I would attract customers that way? Yes, but not the right sort. I've had enough of posing there with the blind open.

I go across and pull down the blind, but not before checking that there is no one staring up at me in the street below. The street is empty, as far as I can tell. This is certainly a lonely apartment. I'm not aware that there are any other residential apartments nearby. What on earth made me decide to come here? It's great in the daytime, but not at night.

I still haven't dropped my Nissan Micra off at the garage where Rupert Forrester works. First thing in the morning I'm phoning Courtney and telling her I'm coming over to Brevelstone with the note and the envelope. It's up to her what she does about it. I'm hoping Detective Inspector Dickinson takes it seriously, and tracks down the perpetrator. I don't want to receive any more notes, and who knows, there might be clues on this one to lead him to the gang.

Chapter 17

Fortunately, nothing else dramatic happened in the night. Nothing that I was aware of, anyway. I'm sitting in Button Up at the corner table which Abi has now agreed will be permanently reserved for family and friends. I feel privileged. Honestly I do. It's great to be accepted in a town that holds some uncomfortable memories – mostly uncomfortable things of my own making. What a timid little thing I must have been!

I'm having a large cappuccino and a croissant with butter and raspberry jam. I guess this is going to be my regular breakfast fare for the next twelve months, six days a week. Button Up is closed on Sundays, and Abi, Melanie and the others deserve a break. Things can get quite busy here, and I admire the way they keep their patience with some of the more demanding customers.

It's only just after eight, but I've already taken the step of phoning Courtney Jacobs' personal phone to explain about the note. At first she tried to dismiss it as some sort of practical joke, until I pointed out that the only people who are likely to know my connection to Sam and my new address are going to be people connected to Sam's murder.

Brevelstone is only an hour or so away, and I'm seeing Courtney at ten thirty at the central police station. She hopes to get Detective Inspector Dickinson with her.

She's not sure he'll take much notice, but surely it has the potential to be a major step forward. Not every criminal thinks like a detective. Some wouldn't realise there could even be DNA on the gum to seal the envelope.

I don't think modern gum is made from cows' hoofs, which of course contain cow DNA. Sorting it out is not my speciality, but forensic experts can do it. If I tell Abi what I'm doing, she'll probably say she hopes no innocent cows get arrested. I'm quickly learning that's just her sort of humour.

I smile to myself, even though I'm not in any mood for joking. I notice Abi hasn't left the folded newspaper on my table. I imagine she wants to have a crack at the cryptic crossword herself, and perhaps impress me when I call in later today and see every square filled.

I'll have to buy the same newspaper and see if I can beat Abi to completing it – without using the internet! Cryptic clues can be addictive. I remember how on the Christmas before last, Sam and I played a game with secret messages written in invisible ink.

We had two silver ballpoint pens filled with fluorescent ink. It was completely invisible under normal lighting, but the pens had a small UV LED in the end that made the writing shine a bright blue. We set each other a cryptic treasure trail and laid out Post-it notes around the house. We had our evening meal, then started the chase. It was great fun, but of course both our trails quickly led to the bedroom. Yes, our minds were as one!

Time is dragging. I don't need to leave for Brevelstone much before half nine, but, yes, I ought to call at the print shop before leaving town. I want to make sure Tom and Daisy are getting a good picture on Tom's phone.

My small table in the corner faces the main coffee shop doorway. I can see a woman who looks to be in her mid to late fifties walking towards the door of Button Up, then turning away and coming back. No, I think she's going to my office door. The problem is, I can't see my door from inside Button Up.

I don't know whether to go out and ask if I can help, or just sit here and see what happens. Perhaps she's going to deliver another printed warning. In that case I think I'll wait. I'm wearing jeans and trainers, and she shouldn't be hard to catch if she delivers a note and runs away. The problem is, I can't see my front door.

I've read just about every Sherlock Holmes story written, and remember how either Sherlock or Watson sees someone outside 221B Baker Street, and even if Holmes doesn't know who it is, he looks at their clothing and their general demeanour, often noting a particular shade of mud on their shoes that is only found in a remote part of Scotland, and immediately deduces who they are and why they're there. But that's fiction, and it all makes sense while I'm reading the stories.

I stand up slowly and go out through the coffee shop doorway. The only way I'll know that she presses my office bell is if I can see her doing it. It's possible to get a video doorbell connected to the wi-fi that will send me a phone signal when it rings. Perhaps I ought to get one, so I can see who the caller is and talk to them even if I'm away on another job. Another job? Chance would be a fine thing, especially one that isn't pro bono.

I'm standing well back, but in a position where I can see what's happening if she goes to my entrance door. I thought she was going away, but she's back now, muttering to herself. She's smartly dressed, and probably not short of money. In other words, the sort of client I eagerly anticipate. She looks harmless enough, and seems to be in some sort of distress. Should I go to her and explain who I am, and ask if I can help?

Before I can come up with the answer that is probably somewhere to be found in one of my detective handbooks, she rings my bell and stays put. Time to reel her in.

If I'd known I was going to get a client, I wouldn't be wearing these casual clothes. My tight black skirt and jacket with white blouse look impressive. I walk forward slowly, so as not to scare her. She's not looking at me, and I don't want to tap her on the shoulder and give her a heart attack. I'm not sure my public liability insurance covers things like that. So I cough, discreetly.

She's still staring at the door, obviously expecting it to open. "Good morning," I say in a gentle sort of voice, "can I help you? I'm Janika Jones."

She turns quickly, and looks frightened. When she sees it's just harmless me, she relaxes. "You're Janika Jones?" she asks, perhaps not believing me the first time. I definitely should have worn my office best.

I get my keys from my pocket and begin to unlock the door. Hopefully, that will help her believe I am who I claim to be. "Would you like to come up?"

She turns around and looks left and right, and then nods. I don't know if she's paranoid or has a serious security problem. Anyway, I'm about to find out because she's following me up the stairs. The automatic spring closure shuts the door behind her and I hear the latch click shut and automatically lock. If she changes her mind about giving me an assignment, she won't be able to escape without my key!

"I'm worried about my daughter," she says quietly, looking around as though afraid of being overheard. "She's involved with a much older man. He says he's single, but I'm not so sure. I'm prepared to pay you well."

Finally, money. This sort of investigation is fairly straightforward for anyone who knows how to do it, and hopefully I do. We did several examples on the residential course. Well, straightforward unless the man or woman in question has changed their name and assumed a completely new identity with a convincing back story. Then it's a job for the police. They have legal access to all bank and social service records.

The woman has given me her name as Mrs Phyllis Miller. "Mrs Miller," I say, "I need to establish one thing before I consider taking on this case. Supposing it turns out that this man is honourable, and is definitely *not* married, but is perhaps legally divorced. Would you still want your daughter to have a relationship with him?"

This is clearly a new thought, and she looks completely taken aback. "Would I?"

I don't say anything. She seems to be talking to herself. She's sitting bolt upright at the moment, staring straight ahead at something over my shoulder. Probably the stockroom window of the shoe shop opposite. I turned the desk round the moment I moved in. Pete came up and gave me a hand.

I think it's important for the client to be facing the daylight, with my face slightly in shadow. It's not as though I'm going to be holding an inquisition, but I feel that having my face in shadow will help the client relax as they share possible confidences. Confidences like concern over a daughter dating an older married man.

"I see what you mean," Phyllis Miller says. "Do I really like Victor Armitage? That's the question, isn't it?"

I nod. "How old is your daughter?" Judging by Mrs Miller's age, she's going to be at least twenty, and therefore a legally consenting adult in any relationship. Except in a bigamous marriage, of course.

Mrs Miller seems to be muttering something to herself, and her eyes are now shut. She's probably wondering whether I'm going to dismiss her concerns as just silly.

"Janika," she says. "May I call you Janika?"

I nod, and she continues. "You've hit the nail on the head exactly. Laura is nearly twenty-three. Victor Armitage is far too old for her. He's at least forty-five, and he's almost bald."

I'm assuming it's the age rather than the lack of hair that's worrying Mrs Miller. Yes, I can certainly see things from her point of view. If I had a daughter of twenty-three, I would want to check up on a much older man, even if he wasn't married.

"So can you do something about it?" Mrs Miller asks.

I tell her my hourly rate, and say it could take several hours work, spread over a few days. Does she want me to go ahead?

I can tell how keen she is for me to dig the dirt on this Victor Armitage, judging by the way she doesn't even hesitate. "Yes," she says almost eagerly, "do it. Do you want me to sign something now?"

I feel obliged to tell her there is no *guaranteed* way to know if someone is married. The term "Marriage" is not as simple as it sounds. There is religious marriage, register office marriage, civil-law marriage, domestic partnership, invalid marriage where the priest or clerk has fraudulent credentials, and other types of marriage in foreign parts. Many legal marriages that are entered into the records in one country may end in divorce in another country without being cross-linked in any records.

Yes, if you want certain benefits, you need to produce proof of marriage. In some cases the court may accept wedding invitations and wedding photos in lieu of a marriagc ccrtificatc as proof of marriage in another country like, say, Madagascar. Yes, I've really taken in a lot from my training, even though I haven't really wanted to get involved in relationship problems.

Often you just have to trust the person from another country to tell you whether they are married or not. There's no international body that keeps records of every marriage in every country every day. But in spite of that, with a bit of luck it can be surprisingly easy. It's much easier to prove someone *is* married than to prove they're *not*. Anyway, I tell Mrs Miller I'm prepared to have a go, although I don't want to give her any false hopes by making any sort of promise.

I look at my spy clock on the wall. I can't afford to let Mrs Miller walk away without signing the contract she seems keen to put her name to, but it means I'm going to miss calling at Tom and Daisy's print shop on my way to Brevelstone to meet Courtney Jacobs. That's okay, I'll phone them as soon as Mrs Miller has gone and tell them to phone me if there's a problem in logging into the clock and getting an image on the shop wi-fi – and I'll do my best to call in some time in the afternoon.

Half an hour later I leave for Brevelstone with my first paid commission. Mrs Miller has given me a generous fee upfront with bank transfer. Much better than getting checks that can bounce. Whoopee, all I have to do now is investigate Mr Victor Armitage to earn my money.

Mrs Miller has done most of the necessary homework for me. She has Victor's address and his place of work. She says he speaks with a local accent, which means he is almost certainly not from Madagascar. A local search of the records may be all I need. Mrs Miller even has full details of his car, and his mobile phone number which she secretly got from her daughter's phone. So no problems that I can see.

As I leave town to join the main road to Brevelstone, I look in the rear-view mirror. That black car has been behind me since I left Button Up. Is *that* going to be a problem?

Chapter 18

I have my camera with me. It's digital, naturally, and compact. The fantastic lens has a surprisingly long zoom range for its size. Thirty times. The lens has exceptional definition, and the chip has so many pixels on it that the image can be enlarged substantially without losing much detail.

Thirty minutes later I'm approaching a place where the main road crosses a river on an old stone bridge. If that car really is following me, and if it's being driven by one of the gang who killed Sam, I'm definitely not going to stop by a bridge! I seem to remember there's a turning to the picturesque village of Cravenwell not far ahead. I'm going to turn off there and see what happens.

I already have a good plan. Assuming the car follows me, I'm going to park in the centre of the village and start taking photographs of the old cottages. And then I'll turn the car around and start to drive back to Button Up. It means I'll have to phone Courtney and explain I'm going to be late, and of course give her the reason.

If anything happens to me on the road, at least she'll know about the problem, and I'll probably have been able to give her the registration number of the black car that's still behind me.

The turning to the village is signposted ahead, and I indicate left and slow right down, giving the black car plenty of warning. To my relief, it passes me just before I make the left turn. I glance up at my dash cam. Yes, it will definitely have recorded the registration plate, although it looks as though I panicked unnecessarily. And even if it's not clear on the dash cam, I've remembered the registration, and immediately dictate it to a small USB recorder I keep in my pocket.

It's illegal to hold a mobile phone while driving a car in England, even if it's only to dictate something and not make a call. So far, the law doesn't include dictating on a device that is independent of a mobile phone. Several items of my extensive range of equipment have already proved to be useful. There's nothing like being well prepared.

What am I going to do now? Well, I've made the left turn, and although the black car hasn't followed me, if I'm quick I can take a few photographs in the village. I can send them to my parents. I'm sure they'll be interested to know what the picturesque countryside is like around where I'm working. I've already sent them a view of the road with Button Up and my sign in the upstairs window, but they haven't got around to commentating on it yet.

I have a good memory for names and numbers, and just in case my dash cam and my USB digital recorder have failed, surely unlikely, I make a written note of the black car's registration number. If I give it to Courtney, she will be able to run it through the police computer if she thinks there's good enough reason to do it.

I'm parked outside a beautiful cottage with a

thatched roof, and some sort of creeper trailing round the ancient oak door. Unfortunately, next to it is a Chinese takeaway. I suppose that's what they call progress. Were there no planners prepared to stop the development? The village pub, *The Three Horseshoes* looks quaint, and definitely worth a photograph. And if I drive on down the road a bit, I can probably take a photograph of the cottage without including the takeaway.

The front of a black car slides slowly to a halt in a side road at the end of the main street. Surely, it can't be. What should I do? Should I pretend I haven't seen it? Should I go there and bang on the window and demand to know why I'm being followed? Would that put me at risk of being bundled inside and kidnapped?

I'm not thinking rationally. It might not even be the same car. Why would it be? There's no one around. This must be the most deserted village in the whole county. The pub is closed, so I can't go in there, although someone might be around. I can see two cars in the car park behind. There's a small general store, which will provide some cover if I need to run for help.

I'm going to walk forward boldly, pretending to take photographs as I go, and read the car's number plate from a safe distance. I feel really stupid for going through all this playacting. Then I remember something from the distance learning course I did. *Be careful, be safe.*

With that wise counsel in mind, I'm walking forward, stopping every now and then to take a photograph. I'm going to take a photograph of the front of the car, because I can't quite see its registration plate clearly enough from here.

I keep walking nearer to the black car. It's an Audi. It hasn't moved since I saw it draw up, and I haven't seen anyone get out of it. I guess the driver is still in there, but I'm not going to even glance at it. I'm acting as if it's of no interest to me at all.

I'm holding my camera at my side as though I'm not about to use it, with my eyes fixed on the other side of the road. I pretend I've seen something interesting in the distance, but I pause just for a moment, and without raising the camera I fire off a sideways picture of the front of the black Audi.

My mouth feels dry. *Be bold, Janika. You have to get used to situations like this. Just pretend this is nothing more than part of your residential training course.*

I walk on a bit further and hold the camera up to photograph another quaint cottage. This one is standing back in a beautifully cared for garden with a wishing well that looks genuine. But instead of taking a photograph I flick back to see what I've already taken. No wonder my mouth feels dry. It's the car that followed me here.

I'm now terrified of being snatched. If only there was someone around. Well, I can see an elderly man staring out from the cottage window. He waves to me, and it seems to be a friendly wave rather than one telling me to mind my own business and clear off.

He comes to the door. He's smartly dressed with a tweed jacket. He's even wearing a tie. My guess is that he's ex-military. "It's a beautiful old well, isn't it," he says. "When my grandparents lived here it was the only source of water they had."

"That's fascinating," I say. "Can I come into the garden and take some photographs? I think it's charming."

"We get lots of visitors," he says. "A lot of people don't believe the well is real." His eyes twinkle. "I assure them it is, but my father declared the well and the water unsafe, and sealed the top."

I know my mouth is dry, very dry, and I'm desperate for a drink, but I share the opinion that the water might be dangerous. It probably was safe okay years ago, but now with so many drains and things around.... "I'm all right for now, thanks."

It occurs to me that the water might never have been safe, not even in times gone by when typhoid was the killer disease. Isn't typhoid a waterborne infection?

"Would you like to come in?" the elderly man asks.

I'm guessing he's lonely. He probably looks out of the window most of the day, hoping to see someone to chat to. I look all around me, but only have one target in mind. The black car. It has moved forward slightly now, and the driver looks as though he's staring at me, although the car is too far away to be sure. Time to set my little camera to maximum zoom.

I have to do this next step carefully. The elderly man comes into the garden to show me the well, and I ask if I can take a photograph of him by it. He looks thrilled at the prospect. As he stands almost rigidly to attention, I pretend to take a couple of photographs of him from one direction, but it has to be a pretence. I'm leaving my camera on full zoom. I point to the thatched roof and ask the man to look up at it.

He doesn't query my request, even though it makes no sense to anyone actually taking a photograph. But as I raise my camera I'm looking at the screen, and there is the black car with a man watching me. The passenger window is wound down, and even though he's in the driving seat on the opposite side of the car that's over a hundred yards away, I'm confident I've got a clear picture of him, and I don't think he's realised what I've done.

I zoom back to a normal angle, and ask the elderly man to pose again so I can take the pictures of him and his well that he thinks I've already taken. It's important to go through this charade. Within what seems like seconds I learn that the old man's name is Wilfred Chadwick. He was a sergeant major in a local army regiment, and his father and grandfather were also in the same regiment. They both won medals, his grandfather in the First World War, and his father in the Second, although his grandfather was killed in France in 1917.

If I have time, he'd like to show me the collection. They both won medals. He's been widowed for the last ten years, and has a married daughter living nearby, although trying to read his body language there's some sort of relationship problem there. Would I like a cup of tea?

Would I? Perfect. I have to phone Courtney and give her the registration number of the car. It's unlikely Wilfred Chadwick will have wi-fi, so I may have to take a photograph of the camera screen with my phone and send her the picture of the driver as an attachment. If she says the quality isn't good enough, I have a suitable lead in my bag in the boot of the Micra to connect the camera and phone together.

Wilfred goes into the tiny kitchen to make us some tea, and I explain I have to make a phone call. He points to his landline. I thank him, but tell him I need to use my own phone because I don't know the number. It all sounds a bit confusing, but he smiles in a way that tells me he's used to being confused, and disappears. I hear a tap running into what sounds like an old-fashioned kettle while I phone Courtney and explain the whole situation.

Ten minutes later, while sipping milky tea from a delicate floral painted bone china cup with a matching saucer that must be at least a hundred years old, my phone rings. It's Courtney, and she has news for me.

Chapter 19

"Janika, thanks for reporting this. We've identified the driver. He's known as Gerry the Taff. He's a small time Welsh crook, well known for selling his services to anyone who wants a bit of surveillance. You did well to spot him. He's obviously not as invisible as he likes to think he is."

I suppose that's good news. "So what am I going to do now? Does it matter if he follows me all the way to Brevelstone central police station?"

I can hear a sharp intake of breath from Courtney. "No, don't do that, Janika. He's not likely to be dangerous, but we don't know who he's working for at the moment. But I assure you we're going to find out. I've managed to contact DI Dickinson, and naturally he's concerned. He approves of the playacting you've done so far, and suggests you return to your office, and perhaps pause to take a few more pictures at various beauty spots on the way back. Gerry the Taff isn't that bright, and he might report back that he's made a mistake and you're just a normal tourist."

"I don't understand how he knew I've stopped here in the village," I say.

Courtney laughs. "He's probably put a tracker on your car."

I shake my head, even though Courtney obviously can't see me. "Not on *my* car. I checked it the other day. Oh!" I feel so stupid. "Before you say anything, Courtney, from now on I'll check it *every* day before I go anywhere. What do you suggest I do? There's no point in trying to lose him on the way back to the office, is there?"

I can hear Courtney still laughing. "You didn't hear this from me, Janika, but why don't you send Gerry the Taff on a wild goose chase? When you park back at your office, just make sure you're not being watched, and find the tracker. You know the sort of places to look for it."

"I can do better than that," I say. "I've got my bug detector in my kit in the back of my Micra. I know what you're going to suggest. I give Gerry the Taff the slip when I get back to town. I'm sure I can do that, and I go into the local supermarket car park. I find the tracker. It's almost certainly going to be magnetic. Then I clip it on the wheel arch of the car parked next to me, and drive off quickly and park in a side road where I'm not likely to be spotted."

"Janika," Courtney says, "how could I possibly suggest you do such a thing? Nothing was further from my mind. No way can I support you doing that."

I don't know if her phone calls are all recorded, so I'm not going to say I'm sure that's exactly what she had in mind. But whether it was or not, it's what I'm going to do.

"So how am I going to get the note and envelope to you if I can't leave town?" Actually, the answer is obvious. "As soon as I ditch the tracker I'll take a more roundabout route to Brevelstone."

"Sounds good, Janika. It's best if you don't come to the station. Where in Brevelstone would you like to meet me?"

Anywhere but Mill Bridge, but I don't say it. I haven't been near that bridge since Courtney took me there and I spotted Sam's gold cross. And I don't intend to go there ever again. "The railway station car park," I say. I know it well. "By the far fence, where they're doing all the building work."

Wilfred Chadwick comes out to his little front garden to wave me goodbye, and tells me to be sure to call again if I'm passing his way, and he can show me the medals and other mementos of the family's military service. He even asks if he can phone me some time. In a quiet voice he tells me that life has been lonely since his wife died seven years ago this month, and although his daughter lives relatively close, he rarely sees her. It seems there's a problem with her son and her husband.

I give him one of my Button Up Detective Agency cards, and assure him I'd love to hear from him. And that's the truth. I would.

From the look in his eyes, it seems I've made a friend for life. Maybe I'll be able to help him in the future if he ever needs a private investigator. But until that happens, it will be good just to chat on the phone. Maybe even call in and have another cup of very milky tea in an ancient cup and saucer.

I glance casually up and down the road. There's no sign of the black Audi, or of Gerry the Taff. Well, if he's put a tracker on my car, he'll be able to find me. That makes me wonder why he bothered to stay so close behind me on the way. The sooner I get back to town and park at the supermarket and switch the tracker onto another car, the sooner I can relax.

In that case, I might as well find the tracker now, assuming there is one. I have my work pack in the back of my car, which includes the bug detector. Not that I was expecting to need it when I set out, but the whole kit fits neatly into a bag divided into compartments. The detector is quite small, and once again I look up and down the road. It's still clear. Not even a man standing on his own. I don't think I'd recognise Gerry the Taff from the photograph I took, although obviously someone in the CID office has managed it with their face recognition technology, combined with their personal knowledge of the man.

The detector lights up immediately. The tracker is clamped inside the left rear wheel arch. I look up and down the road again. Where is Gerry the Taff hiding? Perhaps he's gone home, thinking I really have come here just to take photographs. Courtney said he's not very bright.

At that moment, my phone rings. I recognise the number. It's Brevelstone CID. Courtney Jacobs' phone. I answer it, but all I can hear is Courtney talking in the background. "Hold on, Janika," she says to me, "I'll be with you in a moment."

After what seems quite a lengthy discussion with someone in the office, I hear Courtney's voice on the phone again. "Are you still there, Janika?"

"Yes. What's happened?

"DI Dickinson isn't here at the moment," Courtney says, "but I've had a word with the Detective Sergeant. She is also involved in the case. She doesn't want you coming to Brevelstone with the package. She says it's not worth the risk. She wants you to stay where you are and she's sending a car. Is there anywhere safe you can sit while you're waiting? Not in the car though."

"How long for?"

I can hear Courtney passing the phone over to someone. A pleasant sounding older woman explains that her name is Detective Sergeant Dyer. She's already arranged to dispatch a car and driver to collect the anonymous note and envelope, and she tells me to stay put because Courtney has told her there's probably a tracker on my car.

I don't like to tell her that it isn't there any longer, and while we're talking I have a bright idea. A delivery truck has pulled up just down the road. It has a Brevelstone address and phone number on it. *Brevelstone Speedy Deliveries*. It's probably not going to be stopping for long.

Detective Sergeant Dyer tells me to stay put and keep my phone handy. She's going to phone me back with further instructions. I wander down the road, holding the magnetic tracker out of sight in my hand.

The driver nods to me as I walk past, and I feel obliged to stop. "Nice day to be out," he calls down from his cab window. "Lovely village this. Are you a local girl?"

I suppose I should be used to it by now, getting chatted up by men in lonely places. I'm sure he's harmless. No criminal gang would drive a truck like this in order to abduct me.

I shake my head but don't feel the need to return his friendly grin. "Just visiting," I say, pointing to Wilfred's cottage. "Are you going back to Brevelstone now?"

From his expression, I guess he's thinking this is his lucky day. "Straight back, love. You looking for a lift?"

At least he hasn't asked me if I'd like to go all the way. Oh dear, I've got to stop thinking about men being after one thing. It's not that I have an aversion to men in general, but at the moment I'm finding it hard to trust any man. That is, apart from Abi's Danny. And Pete Wilders of course, and I'm sure Melanie's husband Steve is trustworthy, although I've yet to meet him. But apart from men like that, yes, I have a problem.

"Sorry, I'd love to travel with you, but I've got my car here. But thanks for the offer."

I can see disappointment on his face, so my conclusion was probably the correct one. And for that, he's going to be the recipient of the tracker. I don't need to go to any great lengths to conceal it. He's still in his cab, and the engine is running. He's not going to hear the magnet grab onto the back of his truck.

I wave goodbye, and return to the old cottage where Wilfred is still standing wistfully in his garden. Well, it wasn't the truck driver's lucky day, but it's going to be Wilfred's. He's going to have the joy of making me another cup of milky tea and show me the medals while I wait for the Brevelstone police driver to arrive. This time,

I'll ask him to go easy on the milk.

Half an hour later the police driver has picked up my package, and I'm saying goodbye to my new old gentleman friend. He's obviously reluctant to let me go, but I promise I'll be back. He assures me the kettle will always be on for me whenever I'm coming this way.

I feel so sorry for him. It's hard enough to lose the partner when you're young, but after a lifetime together, things must get so desperately lonely if you don't have family close by.

I need to get home. Home? Yes, the Button Up Detective Agency is *my* new home. I've only been there a short time, but the whole place has a comfortable, healing feeling. There's something about Abi Button, as was, that brings me peace. Maybe it's because she goes to church. Not that I'm ever going with her. Yes, I went with Sam, even though it wasn't my sort of thing. I felt obliged to go with him as a sort of duty, out of love.

There's just one thing I have to do on the drive back. I must remember to keep a close eye on my rear-view mirror for the black Audi – every single mile of the way.

Just as I'm climbing back in, I can see a black car stopping further down the road. My trick failed. Gerry the Taff isn't chasing the truck all the way to Brevelstone. He's parked two hundred yards down the road, and he's waiting for me to move off. Nice try, Janika.

Chapter 20

I've decided to drive back to town, stopping occasionally to take a few photographs. I'm not going to try to lose my tail. I can do it easily, assuming there was only the one tracker on the car. Oh no! Have I fallen for an elementary trick? Well, it's not important. I'm going to park in my slot behind Button Up and walk to the print shop. After doing another sweep for a possible second tracker.

I'm nearly back, and I haven't seen the black Audi for some time. My phone rings on my hands-free. It's a number I recognise. "Hi, Courtney. Any news?"

I can hear Courtney chuckling. "You'll be glad to know that Gerry the Taff has been picked up by your local police. It seems he was tailing you, but he's been stopped to have his licence and insurance checked. It seems there's a problem, so his car will be temporarily impounded."

"How's he going to get back to Brevelstone?" As I ask the question, I start to laugh. I picture the man standing by the side of the road, thumbing for a lift. Well, it's his fault, especially if his paperwork isn't in order.

"They are holding him until DS Dyer can get there to question him. And while his car is in the pound," Courtney continues, "it will get a good going over. I gather they're expecting to find drugs. He's only a small time dealer, but that's how he supports himself from day to day. Plus doing odd jobs for whoever needs his services. He's not going to trouble you anymore today. What did you do with the tracker? We're going to need it to see if we can find the owner. Gerry the Taff wasn't working for himself, that's for sure."

I laugh. "If you go to Brevelstone Speedy Deliveries, you'll find it clamped to the back of one of their trucks."

I've just pulled into my parking place at the rear of Button Up, and I'm keen to find out if there really *is* another tracker. There isn't. So Gerry the Taff must have seen my car, and guessed what I'd done. In that case he's not as dim as Courtney thinks. Next call, the print shop.

Tom is there, and he looks agitated when he sees me. There's no sign of Daisy.

"It worked," he says. "It actually worked."

I'm pleased to hear that, although why is he using the past tense? Is it broken?

"I'm glad you're here," Tom goes on. "Will everything have been recorded?"

"Only the last eight hours. What's happened?"

"I came to work first," Tom says. "We have to open up at nine, and Nan doesn't always get there in time for both of us to leave. As soon as I got here, I logged in and started looking on my phone at our living room. It's amazing. I could see and hear Daisy and Nan talking together, and then Daisy said goodbye, after giving Katie a kiss."

I'm starting to feel impatient. I hope Tom isn't only telling me this because he loves the technology. "And then something happened?" This is pro bono, and I have a paying assignment for Mrs Miller to check on her daughter's boyfriend called Victor Armitage.

"Too true something happened," Tom says. "The front window is slightly open, and as soon as I hear Daisy drive off, Katie starts to scream. And then it starts. Because she won't stop, Nan starts to shake her. Shakes her violently. The sort of shaking that can damage a young brain. Then she drags Katie out of the room and I can hear them going upstairs. Two minutes later I can hear Nan moving around in the kitchen, and Katie is still screaming from somewhere. She's obviously locked into her bedroom. Then Nan comes back with a cup of tea and sits down and watches the television. And I can hear Katie still screaming in her bedroom."

I really don't know how I should be feeling. Elation that my spy system has been successful, or should I identify with the trauma that the whole family must now be going through?

"Daisy went straight back when I told her what had happened. The thing is, we don't know whether to inform the police or treat it as a family matter. Whatever, Nan is never going to be allowed to see Katie on her own again. Ever. Maybe never even *see* her again."

I can only nod in understanding.

"So if you have the time to call in today, can you get the clock? And if you have a clear recording on the memory card, we would like it. To tell you the truth, Janika, just looking at that clock is going to upset us."

So my first official job has been successful, but how

much better it would have been if the clock had stayed there for several days, and recorded the grandmother playing happily with Katie, and generally having fun.

While we've been chatting, a customer has arrived, and clearly Tom doesn't want to discuss the matter any more. I tell Tom to phone Daisy and get her to switch the recorder off on the back of the clock, so the evidence doesn't get overwritten. I promise to call in sometime late afternoon, but I have another job to do first. Tom says he quite understands, and until they can arrange other childcare, Katie will be at home.

As I leave, I pull the stand holding my flyers and cards even further forward. I don't feel guilty. I've done the family a great favour. No wonder I'm feeling hungry. It's nearly one o'clock. I hurry to Button Up for my lunch. The table in the far corner that I normally sit at is occupied by a man in a smart suit. It's Abi's husband, Danny. Just the man I need to see.

"Hi, Danny," I say. I point to the empty chair at the table. "May I?"

Danny jumps to his feet to help me sit down. He's a gentleman. Abi has a real winner here.

"Can we talk business for a moment?" I ask. Danny glances up at the clock above the service counter. He only has a cup of coffee, so I guess he's already eaten. "I need to pick your brains."

"No problem, Janika, but you'll have to be quick."

I tell him about Mrs Miller, her daughter Laura, and Victor Armitage. He smiles ruefully. "The old, old problem. There's no place where you can register that you're *un*married, only married. And it's difficult to prove a negative. That's not going to help you, I know."

Abi comes across, and pulls up a spare chair. She's not come to take my order, she's come to listen.

"Are you discussing marriage?" she asks, giving me a nudge.

"It's a case Janika is working on," Danny says. "The mother thinks her daughter is being enticed into a relationship by an older married man, but of course she might just be jealous, or maybe has someone already in mind that her daughter can't stand."

Abi gets up and takes my order. A tuna and sweetcorn panini with side salad. Obviously the conversation wasn't as interesting as she hoped.

Danny says he has to leave, and I'm left alone with my thoughts. I'm feeling so sorry for Tom and Daisy, and perhaps even more sorry for little Katie. It's just as well I called at the print shop to get my printing done. I'm the only private investigator in town. So where are all my clients?

A light bulb pops on above my head. Not a real one, but the sort in comic strips. Mrs Miller has already given me details of Victor's house, and even mentioned his smart red VW Golf. I know what a honey trap is, and this plan doesn't involve anything underhand like that. I'm not going to make myself available to him, to see if he can be trusted in a steady relationship with someone else. Definitely not. Probably not.

I insist on paying for my lunch, and as soon as I finish my cappuccino I'm in my Micra, driving to Victor's address. Like many of the roads here in Craidlea, Beechcroft Road isn't one I know, but I have satnav on my phone. It leads me to a smart area, with a row of modern detached houses set well back. Everything looks expensive, including the landscaped gardens.

There's no red Golf on the drive, but it could be in the garage. So I can't tell if Victor Armitage is home. I need an excuse to ring the doorbell, and this is where my brilliant plan comes in. I stop on the other side of the road, jump out, and open the bonnet of my Micra.

I pretend to poke about at the engine, and then gaze around as though seeking help. My old Nissan Micra looks like the sort of car that would break down. I've still not taken it to Rupert's garage to get the door mended and have a full service. Victor's house is on the other side of the road.

I can see an older woman pushing her net curtains aside in the house I'm parked outside, which isn't what I need. Amazingly, I spot a man in the house that I've identified as Victor's. I give him a little wave, but I don't beckon him out. I need to see how he responds to a maiden in distress. Some maiden!

"Can I help you?"

Not only has he come out of the right house, but he answers Mrs Miller's description. This has to be Victor Armitage – mid forties, wealthy looking and smart. And by the way he's walking, he knows it. I can see why any woman, even a naïve young one, would be attracted to him. Except me, of course.

"It keeps happening," I say. "It will start again in a

few minutes. Something to do with the petrol feed, so I've been told. No, I'm fine, but thanks for asking."

I don't want to put him off, but I want to play hard to get, especially if he has something nefarious in mind.

"You can come in and wait if you like. Tea or coffee?"

No honey trap, no honey trap, I say to myself. *And whatever happens, don't get involved with the man, even if it means losing Mrs Miller as a client.* I smile. "That's fine, thanks. I'd rather not, unless your wife is home." I point to his left hand and give a little giggle.

My play acting seems to be working. He studies his hand briefly. "I'm not married. What makes you think that?"

"Isn't that mark where you normally wear a ring?" I can't see any mark, but I'm sure it's all right to say something like that, because I'm working for a client. And anyway, there's no way I'm going to get romantically involved.

Victor laughs. "Definitely no wife."

"A good-looking man like you?" I can feel my heart pounding. The next question is vital. "Steady girlfriend?"

"Not really," he says, and I can see a sort of hunger in his eyes. But I'm not done yet.

"I can't believe it. Your wife must have lost a real treasure when you got divorced."

Am I really saying this? Well, the worst that can happen is that he goes in and slams the door, and I have to give Mrs Miller a refund.

But he doesn't go indoors. "Are you interested?" he asks, with a smirk.

I've been careful to keep my left hand out of sight. "I expect you say that to all the girls." And I laugh. "We don't know each other yet. You're clearly a man of mystery."

I realise that the elderly woman who had been peeping from behind her net curtain has now come out. She's fiddling with one of the ornamental bushes in her front garden. She's obviously ear-wigging.

Victor winks at me, and nods towards the elderly woman. "Why don't you come in and we can get to know each other better?"

I hear the elderly woman making a tutting noise. This is working out well. "I'm in a bit of a hurry," I say. Then I add, "Today."

"That's up to you," he says. Now *he's* playing hard to get.

"Let me just try the engine again." I jump back into my Micra and crank the engine. It fires first time. I get out to slam the bonnet shut, and smile at Victor Armitage. The elderly neighbour is glaring at me as though I've turned up here as the most scarlet of scarlet women, looking for customers.

As I get ready to drive off, I wind down the passenger window and give Victor a wave. "See you," I call out.

Victor returns my wave. "Soon, I hope," are the last words I hear. What a sleazy man. No wonder Mrs Miller is suspicious of him.

The elderly woman lives at number eleven. I need to find out her name before I come back, without my car, wearing one of my disguises.

Chapter 21

I'm back at my office, sitting at my impressive desk with my less than impressive laptop. I really do need something with a brighter screen and a faster hard drive. This one's over three years old, and slow with it. My only concern is getting everything safely transferred to the new one. Some of my favourite apps may not even work. Phone shop guy seems helpful. If I buy a new laptop, perhaps he can transfer everything. I'll have to check when I go to see if he's run out of my business cards.

I'm doing a search for number eleven Beechcroft Road. It's an outside chance, because the resident's name isn't going to be on Google or any news channel unless they've done something noteworthy. Now, that's an idea. I should have thought of it before.

I should be searching for Victor Armitage's name at number fourteen Beechcroft Road. He's much more likely to have done something noteworthy, probably something dodgy. The local paper might even have mentioned his divorce. I'm only assuming he's married, or was married once.

I'm out of luck. Well, I can't expect too much. Just finding Victor Armitage in and being able to chat him up – correction, letting *him* chat *me* up – has been an excellent start. My next port of call will be the main library in town. No, my next visit is going to be Button Up for a large cappuccino and an apple Danish. I need to revive my flagging spirits. The episode with Victor Armitage has drained me, but only temporarily. Plus, I'm still reeling from the distressing story from Tom and Daisy MacDonald with little Katie.

What a day I'm having!

Abi is there, and so is Melanie. Pete appears from the stockroom and the three of them make a beeline for my little table which now has a permanent Reserved sign on it. As Abi has already told me, the Reserved sign means it's reserved for family and friends, and it's great to be accepted so soon as a friend.

"Well?" the three ask, almost in unison.

I need to keep my voice down. The coffee shop is busy with shoppers recovering from their shopping trips. Button Up isn't on the main high street, but it's better than anything I've managed to find in the centre.

"Progress," and that's all I'm going to tell them for now. But then again, as long as I don't mention names, the customers may ask Abi and Melanie who I am when I've left, and they can hand them one of my flyers which are now prominently displayed on the service counter – assuming they haven't picked one up already. "Excellent progress," I add loudly enough for everyone to hear.

"There's very little to tell you at the moment," I say quietly, and Pete immediately loses interest and goes to rescue a toasty.

"I can't discuss it here, but I need to visit a little old lady. I think she's the eyes and ears of the neighbourhood."

Well, I can visit the little old lady once I know her name. I don't want to turn up unannounced. Anyway, Victor Armitage might well be looking from his window. I think he might also fancy himself as the eyes and ears of the neighbourhood, even if it's only to spot local talent. Oh, am I really that cynical about men?

The main library will have what's called the Electoral Roll, which lists every house and resident over the age of eighteen. There's just one drawback to this. By law, it's possible not to have your name included in the public copy of the Electoral Roll, although the council are obliged to keep a secure record of everyone's names. One reason to keep your name secret is if you don't want canvassers and doorstep salespeople turning up and addressing you by name, or sending you personally addressed junk mail. Or even trying to track you down.

Fortunately, the little old lady at number eleven has no reason to conceal her name from public gaze. She is Stephanie Cooke, with an e. As soon I'm outside the library I try directory enquiries on my phone. Not only does Stephanie Cooke have no objection to keeping her name on the public Electoral Role, it seems she's happy to have her phone number listed.

I'm not going to phone her here in the street. I have to go back to Button Up to make the phone call in the privacy of my office which is only a ten minute walk away. I also need to prepare myself for the visit. What colour wig shall I wear?

I sink into one of the small leather armchairs by the

window with my phone. Being a private detective is exhausting, emotionally as well as physically. Mostly emotionally so far.

"Mrs Cooke, my name is Janika Jones. I'm a private investigator and you saw me this morning talking to your neighbour, Victor Armitage."

A loud voice says, "I'm sorry, I don't want——"

"Please hear me out, Mrs Cooke. You're not going to get involved at all, but I represent a mother who is very concerned for her daughter." Maybe that will loosen the old lady's tongue.

"What do you want to know ... exactly?"

"It will be better if I can call in and see you. It's easier to discuss things face-to-face."

I get the impression that Stephanie Cooke has plenty of things she'd like to share about Victor Armitage, and merely needs a bit of encouragement. If I'm talking to her in her house rather than on the phone, I feel certain she'll tell me things I want to know. Also, she won't be able to put the phone down if she feels she's said too much.

"No, no, that won't do," she says. "I don't want Mr Armitage thinking I'm gossiping about him. If he recognises you, he'll guess why you're here. I don't like him, but I have to live here. Sorry."

I'm losing her. "Mrs Cooke, I'm a private investigator. I will come in disguise. You won't recognise me, and nor will Victor Armitage. And I won't bring my car. I'll come in a taxi, and I'll bring a large bunch of flowers as a gift. You can ask me in and I'll let the taxi go. Please, I can't give my clients name, but she is a mother who is seriously concerned about a relationship her daughter is in with Mr Armitage."

Stephanie Cooke says, "Ah, that will be the blonde girl with the black sports car who sometimes spends the night. And her already married as well. Yes, if you really are a private investigator, there are certainly things I would like to tell you. When can you come? You can come now if you like. Mr Armitage is out, and he never gets back until after four thirty. I don't like to gossip, but he'll be at the betting shop."

The "blonde girl with the black sports car who sometimes spends the night" doesn't sound like Mrs Miller's Laura, which could be good news for Mrs Miller, but not for her daughter. And "her already married as well" implies that Victor Armitage is also married.

Knowing that people who "don't like to gossip," are the very ones who do, I'm certain I'm on a winner here with Stephanie Cooke. Time to phone for a cab.

I ask the driver to stop at the filling station where I spot a range of floral arrangements in buckets outside. I'm not going to go to a florist and spend a fortune. I've no idea how fruitful Stephanie Cooke is going to prove to be. But I'll buy one of their better bunches, and peel the garage sticker off the cellophane packaging.

I'm wearing a long ginger wig that comes to my shoulders. Thinking about it now, perhaps I should have waited and brought Liam with me. We'd look like mother and son visiting a relation. But Liam isn't back from school yet, and I certainly don't want a young boy listening to what might be a rather sordid conversation.

It's a warm day, so I'm wearing a mid-length floral skirt instead of the jeans I was wearing earlier, and a fawn jacket and high heels. As I totter up the driveway towards Stephanie Cooke's house wearing a pair of spectacles with thin black frames and plain glass, I can see her standing in the window. And she's frowning. She obviously doesn't recognise me. Brilliant.

Even now, when she's come to the door, she's still frowning. She looks at the flowers. "Are you sure you've got the right house, dear?"

I smile. "It's me, Janika Jones. We spoke on the phone just a few minutes ago."

She's peering at me. Either my disguise is amazing, or her eyesight isn't that special. It doesn't matter about her eyesight, as long as it's been good enough to keep an eye on Mr Armitage.

She looks at my business card and smiles. "Yes, of course you did. And what lovely flowers you've brought me, dear. I've been expecting you. I'm sure you'd like tea."

I'm not sure if she means a cup of tea, or what some elderly people call afternoon tea, consisting of sandwiches and cake. I'm happy for either. It's all in the cause of duty. So I say, "Yes please."

"I'll just put these in water, dear," Mrs Cooke says, and disappears into the back of the house, leaving me standing in the hallway.

I can hear the sound of running water, and guess she's filling a vase. After a moment there's more running water, and this sound has an echo with it. My detective brain tells me she's now filling a kettle. Well, it's just a guess.

It seems I'm right, because Stephanie Cooke reappears with the flowers in a vase and she tells me the kettle is on. She'd like me to follow her back into the kitchen.

"Sorry to leave you standing, dear. Thoughtless of me. Now, why are you here? It seems to have slipped my mind."

Fortunately, I'm not going to need Stephanie Cooke as a court witness. She'd be totally at sea, and probably unable to remember anything about what she had earlier claimed to have seen. But I'm not after a robust court witness who won't break down during aggressive cross examination, just someone who doesn't mind indulging in a bit of gossip.

Chapter 22

"I'm so sorry to hear you have a neighbour like Mr Armitage," I say, opening the conversation as soon as we're sitting down with a tray containing a fancy teapot, two delicate cups in matching saucers, a milk jug and the sugar bowl. Plus an assortment of rather plain looking biscuits. It seems that elderly people love their delicate china, as well as their biscuits. I don't think a delicate tea service like this would last long with my rather rough and ready washing-up.

"I never want to speak ill of anybody," Stephanie Cooke says quietly, as though afraid of being overheard by her neighbour on the opposite side of the road. "It's just that I don't like to see women getting hurt."

"Nor do I," I say, with some emphasis. Been there, done that. Bruno nearly ruined my life in Poland. Six slow and deliberate blows to my stomach. I counted every one. The bleeding started almost immediately.

"Here's my business card, Mrs Cooke. Are you *Mrs* Cooke?" I can see a ring on her arthritic fingers, but there's no sign of a man in the house.

"Mr Cooke passed away three years ago," she says, a sad look in her eyes. "I'm not here for much longer."

What's the right response? I say, "I'm sorry to hear that. I have to say you look well."

Stephanie Cooke laughs for the first time. "I'm not joining my husband just yet," she says, "but this house is too big for me. My daughter insists I go to live with her, but I don't want to impose. Anyway, enough of me. So you're investigating Mr Armitage?"

"I am. It is all right if we record this conversation? It will only be between us and my client."

"Yes of course, dear, if you need to. It's quite like playing detectives."

She's right. This is just the sort of role playing we did at my residential course. But now I'm doing it for a living. I've already switched my recorder on. That's important, in case the person being interviewed denies you ever asked for permission. If they say no, then I can just switch it off. No harm is done, and they won't know they've been recorded for just a few seconds.

"As I said on the phone, I can't give you any names, but a mother is concerned about her daughter's relationship with Mr Armitage. From the description you gave of the visitor with the dyed blonde hair with the black sports car who sometimes stays the night, we're not talking about the same woman."

"Well, that's the only one I've seen here. Could you describe your client's daughter?"

Actually, I can't. All I know is her name and age. "She's in her early twenties. Does that help?"

Mrs Cooke shakes her head. "I knew it, I knew it. I always suspected he had several women on the go. This visitor is at least the same age as Mr Armitage. She is what we used to call mutton dressed as lamb. Flashy. I don't know what she sees in him, or what he sees in her."

"My client is concerned that Mr Armitage may be discussing marriage with her daughter. I want to be honest with you, Mrs Cooke. What I did this afternoon was part of a ploy. My car didn't really break down. I wanted to get into conversation with Victor Armitage to see if I could get him to admit he's married. My client's daughter believes he's single."

"Do drink your tea, dear," Mrs Cooke says. "Definitely married. I don't listen to people's conversation, of course not, but I was in the garden and I couldn't help overhearing that brazen hussy with the dyed hair and dark roots asking him when his divorce is going to come through."

I take a delicate sip of tea from the delicate bone china cup and return it safely to the saucer. "And what did he say?"

"The man said he still hadn't done anything about it, but it didn't bother him if it didn't bother her. And then they both laughed. What sort of people are living in the world nowadays?"

Probably the same sort of people who have always been living in the world, but that's only my thoughts, and I make a suitably sympathetic noise. Like Wilfred Chadwick's tea in the village, Mrs Cooke has put far too much milk in my cup. I'm sure I won't do this when I'm old. I prefer tea black to tea that's unnecessarily milky.

"His wife left him three years ago, dear. I do know that."

"Do you know her name?"

"Trish. Something like that. Yes, Tricia. She's still in town, so Mrs Markham says. Living in the Lister area. I expect Mrs Markham will know her address. She knows everything and everyone around here. Would you like me to ask? She lives next door but one."

I shake my head. I expect Mrs Markham has net curtains, too. "Not at the moment thank you, Mrs Cooke. I'm employed by a concerned mother. I have to ask if she requires more information. In that case, I'll definitely come back to you. You've been so helpful. But please don't say anything about my visit to Mr Armitage."

I can be on my way. Two cases in twenty-four hours. Actually, my *only* two cases, but surely those flyers will bring in more work. It's not proof, but I'm hoping Mrs Miller will be able to convince her daughter she's dating a loser when I write my report on what I've seen and heard today, and I won't need to trawl through marriage and divorce records for evidence.

What *is* proven is the result of the surveillance of Tom McDonnell's grandmother and little Katie.

I'm just about to leave, when Mrs Cooke says, "That brazen hussy will be here today. She's always here on a Wednesday at five. If your client wants to come round, she's welcome to sit here in my lounge and watch. She'll be quite safe behind my net curtains."

I think Abi would say spying on neighbours is exactly what net curtains were designed for, and why they still sell well in certain neighbourhoods. I say I'll pass the offer on.

Mrs Cooke suggests it might be unwise for my client's

daughter to come as well, if she and Mr Armitage know each other. "Unless she enters my house secretly. I can leave the back gate open if your client likes. It's no good coming by the front door. If Victor Armitage is looking out of his window, he'll know the game is up."

"That's really good thinking, Mrs Cooke. Anyway, my work here is done for now. I need to report back to my client. Is it all right if I give her your phone number? I expect she'd like to take up your offer of sitting here later to watch the lady arrive."

I phone for a cab, and five minutes later, the milky tea still coating my palate, I'm saying goodbye to Stephanie Cooke.

I phone Phyllis Miller and give her all the details about Stephanie Cooke and the invitation to enter by the back gate with Laura if she wants to spy on Victor Armitage. Mrs Miller thanks me and says she will decide whether to take Laura with her or not, but she certainly intends to be there when the woman with the black sports car turns up at five o'clock. From the way in which she's talking, I'm envisaging a punch-up in the road outside, which should certainly get a few net curtains twitching.

Unless Phyllis Miller subsequently requests my presence at Stephanie Cooke's house, I'm done for the day. This may not be the end of things. If Mrs Miller wants me to find a marriage certificate, or divorce papers, it's time-consuming and going to be expensive unless I know the time and date where these things were registered.

I wouldn't complain if she asked me to proceed, but

for her sake I hope her daughter Laura sees sense when she discovers that she is being two-timed by Victor Armitage.

I mustn't forget to collect my clock from the MacDonalds' house this evening, but now I'm going back to the office to recover. I also have to start writing my report on how I set the camera up at the MacDonalds' house, with a full specification of the camera used, in case there are any subsequent legal complications. And I'll have to make a DVD from the memory card when I get it, for Tom and Daisy to keep.

I don't know why, but whenever I return to my office, I feel compelled to call into Button Up first. Perhaps I'm hoping there will be a client there, waiting for me to return, or Abi or someone will have a secret message that a visitor doesn't want to commit to writing or pass on in a phone call. Some sort of coded phone number or something.

Oh, I'm tired. Working as a private investigator clearly isn't all it's cracked up to be. I have to learn not to get caught up in my client's emotions. I have to be cool, calm and collected. But I'm not built that way. Having suffered physically and emotionally for several years in Poland, I can identify only too readily with other people's hurt. Maybe that's why I've taken this up as a career. To protect the innocent and the vulnerable.

As I enter Button Up, I freeze in the doorway. I recognise that balding head and wispy moustache. What is Detective Inspector Dickinson doing here, unannounced? The cheek of the man!

Chapter23

DI Dickinson jumps to his feet. He's wearing dark jeans and a lightweight navy blue bomber jacket. It would be easy to assume he's come here informally, but this is how detectives dress when they're working. It's how Sam dressed. Detectives don't want to advertise who they are. They leave that to the uniformed police.

Danny Wells, of course, has to wear his own version of uniform, a slate grey very expensive-looking suit, because he *does* want to advertise who he is. As Abi has reminded me several times, he's a young lawyer with a promising future at Branks, Davis & Waters.

"Janika," DI Dickinson calls, as he comes across to me, knocking into one of the tables and almost upsetting a nearly full glass of coke. The woman who is sitting there with her child grabs hold of it just in time.

I've no idea why the detective inspector is here, and I'm certainly not going to rush into his arms like old-time friends.

"We need to have a chat, Janika," he says, turning briefly to apologise to the woman with the quick reactions. "Can we go up to your office?" the detective inspector says. "I've got some news I want to share. And don't forget, please call me Roger."

Well, that's what the office is for. I'm assuming he's here for work, not for romance. "Come on up." My keys are in my bag, and I beckon him outside. We've become the centre of attention for both customers and staff. I can see Pete raising his eyebrows at Abi, and grinning. No matter, I would probably have done the same at his age. No I wouldn't. Bruno had already broken my spirit by the time I was Pete's age. And it took me nearly six more years to finally summon up the courage to break free and return to England. Crazy.

I want to keep this visit on a formal footing, but I nod. Anyway, calling him Roger isn't going to hurt. I can't believe he's here with passionate intentions.

I unlock the street door and reach to unset the alarm. For some reason, I manage to block what I'm doing by keeping my head in the way of the keypad. I've no idea why. Just something seems a little bit off. I tell Roger to go on ahead. I'm still uncomfortable with men following me closely up the stairs.

Roger makes suitable noises to indicate he's *still* impressed by my office. Well, that is *still* all he's going to see. I point towards the leather armchairs by the window and invite him to sit down. I'm not going to make him tea or coffee. He's probably drunk more than enough coffee down below, and I really don't want him invading my living quarters to use my toilet. Hopefully, he thought of that before I arrived.

"Busy, Janika?"

"Two interesting surveillance jobs," I explain. "Both completed satisfactorily from the client's point of view, although the people on the other end are clearly going to be upset. I can't let that affect me. I've righted two wrongs, and that makes me feel good ... Roger. I'm sure you've not come all the way from Brevelstone to see my office again. I imagine you have something special to tell me."

He's nodding. "Look, Janika, we're on the verge of a breakthrough. Thank you for sending us that note and envelope. I'm sorry you had to go to so much trouble. If I'd been in the office, I would have sent a car immediately, and saved you the kerfuffle."

"Did Gerry the Taff tell you anything interesting?"

Roger Dickinson frowns and raises a finger. "Best not to discuss it here, Janika," he says. And he leans across and touches my knee as he speaks. Then he seems to realise what he's done and draws back quickly. But he doesn't apologise.

I swing my legs a little further away, and try to ignore what's just happened. This is a man whose family have left him, according to Detective Constable Courtney Jacobs. Perhaps he's lonely. Well, if so, he's not getting any comfort here.

"I can assure you, Detective Inspector, this whole apartment is completely safe. I've done a full bug sweep. Nothing." I've decided to call him Detective Inspector from now on, just so he realises we're still on a formal footing. I probably made a stupid mistake in calling him Roger.

He's shaking his head, and I can see a slightly superior smile on his face. "I'm sure you appreciate, Janika, from the training you did, that nowhere is completely safe for confidential discussions. Just ask the British embassy in Moscow!"

I realise I shouldn't have mentioned Gerry the Taff. Presumably that's the mistake I've made. "Sorry," I say meekly. After all, I am in the presence of an experienced Inspector of the CID.

There's a small table close to the armchairs with a notepad on it, so I can quickly make notes should I be lucky enough to get a client. DI Dickinson pulls a pen from his pocket and writes in capitals: WE NEED TO TALK PRIVATELY OUTSIDE.

Then he puts his finger to his lips and shakes his head, as though telling me not to comment aloud. So, using my own pen, I write: WHY?

He points to the door at the top of the stairs and stands up. I have to make a decision quickly. If he has information relating to Sam's death, and his possible killers, then of course I have to go with him. If he's looking for a stand-in wife, then I'm staying put.

He writes: THIS IS IMPORTANT. TO DO WITH YOUR HUSBAND.

Okay, I might as well do as he suggests. I nod, and get up and go to the door at the top of the stairs.

He's shaking his head and pointing to my phone. From the way he's waving his hands, he wants me to leave it behind. I frown and shake my head, and open my hands in a sort of despairing gesture.

"Bugs," he mouths silently.

Naturally, we didn't do lip-reading on my residential course, but I can usually manage to catch just one word at a time. I want to tell him that there aren't any bugs on my phone. It's been fully checked by phone shop guy – unless of course he put one on there. It would be foolish to think he's part of the gang that killed Sam. I'm not going to get into an argument, so I place my phone on the desk. Perhaps it's a sensible thing to do, if Detective Inspector Dickinson is going to name names.

I wave DI Dickinson to go ahead of me, but he needs the keys to be able to open the door to the street.

We are out in the street and I've locked the second security lock after setting the alarm. It seems that DI Dickinson approves of all my security measures. Actually, I'm feeling proud of how well I thought things through. I don't want an irate grandmother or a sleazy Romeo breaking in and berating me for daring to spy on them. And perhaps even angrier visitors storming up the stairs.

"This is awkward," Roger Dickinson says. I'm thinking of him as Roger again now we're out in the open. "The thing is, Janika, I don't want to raise any attention to ourselves. Is it all right if I put my arm around your shoulder so we look like friends?"

"Definitely not," I say firmly, whilst trying to make my response sound friendly.

I'll say that for him, he backs off immediately. "What I have to show you is beyond confidential," he says. "There can be no possibility of being overheard or even watched. I noticed the small park at the far end of this road. Perhaps we can go there to talk."

Danger signals are popping up in my head, but only small ones at this stage. My self defence training will come in handy, should it be needed. And I'm sure it won't be. Roger Dickinson may be missing his family, but I can't believe he's entertaining any romantic fantasies of moving in with me.

"The benches are well spaced out," Roger says. "I'm sure we'll find an empty one without any bushes behind us."

I'm about to say, "Anywhere, as long as it's not near any bridges," but that would be tasteless as well as tactless. The detective inspector only has my welfare in mind.

That's good, there are four empty benches out of the five in the park. A woman with a child in a buggy is feeding the pigeons on one, and that would seem the safest bench to sit near. I didn't need to be trained to work that one out.

A scruffy man with a newspaper has come in after us and goes to sit down on a bench on the other side of the park. He has a nearly empty beer bottle that he puts on the bench by his side. He's probably drunk, but I don't think he's likely to bother us.

"The thing is, Janika," Roger Dickinson says as we settle ourselves down, "information from Gerry the Taff, plus finding his prints on the envelope of the threatening note you got, has led him to enter a plea bargaining proposal. We found other prints on the note, besides yours, Janika."

I force a laugh. "I hope you're not here to arrest me, Roger."

He shakes his head and looks serious. "We don't know who the other prints belong to yet, and they may have no connection with the gang – but Gerry the Taff doesn't know that. He knows a lot more than he's telling us, but he's scared, and wants to go into our witness protection programme and be off the streets."

Roger points to a large beech tree on the edge of the park that the council have recently lopped. "Gerry the Taff is a minor player. You don't kill a tree by chopping off branches here and there. We need to kill the tree by destroying the roots, and Gerry obviously has some worthwhile information to share."

The man with the beer seems to be reading a newspaper. He drains the bottle and tosses it into the undergrowth behind the bench.

Trust us to end up in the park with a drunk. I hope he keeps to himself, but at least I have Roger Dickinson with me if there's going to be trouble. Surely I don't need to be afraid.

"I want to level with you, Janika," Roger says. "About my wife and children leaving me."

It's not only the man with a newspaper who's making me feel uneasy. I hate to think where this is going.

"They haven't *really* left me," Roger says quietly. "I was afraid my family's lives would be threatened in connection with this case. I have an aunt in Scotland. We discussed it, and between my wife and me we decided that the most sensible thing was for them to stay there, and not leave a written forwarding address. And then, when your husband was killed, I knew I'd done the right thing."

He points to his mobile phone. "I phone them a couple of times a day. It's probably an over-the-top reaction, but I put word around that we had split, so if the gang find out, they won't see making a threat to my family as a major objective."

I'm too embarrassed to say I was worried that he might be visiting me specially to see if I was interested in a relationship. Stupid, stupid me. No man is going to be interested in me, a widow with a violently aborted baby and a damaged womb that might not be able to bear another child. Yes, stupid, stupid me.

Not that it worried Sam. I told him all about it before our relationship became serious, and he promised he loved me just as I was. The past was the past, he said, and it was only the present and our future that mattered. And when the right time came for us to talk about having a family, Sam assured me he would arrange the very best consultant we could afford for advice and possible treatment. So unless Sam shared these details at work, Roger Dickinson won't know.

The man is still sitting on the opposite bench. He's managed to produce another bottle from somewhere, and it's already nearly empty. He now seems more interested in us than his newspaper.

"We need to go somewhere quieter," Roger says. "Somewhere where we're not going to be interrupted. I've got some photographs on my phone I want you to see. You might recognise someone. What's through the gate at the other end of the park?"

We are too late. The woman and the child have gone and it's just us and the stranger. He's coming across unsteadily, and smiling as though he's going to ask us the time, or more likely for money.

Without turning to look at the man again, I say, "Roger, I think we're in trouble."

"Already on it," Detective Inspector Dickinson says. "Leave it with me. I know how to handle it."

I hope he really *does* know how to handle it. This is looking bad. Then it occurs to me. The two men are in it together! No wonder Detective Inspector Dickinson wanted to come to this particular park to talk. I'm going to die. The detective inspector wouldn't have wanted to kill me in my office, because everyone knows he'd gone up there with me. But in the morning, someone's dog is going to find my body in the bushes and start barking. So, so clever.

"Stand up and start walking," the man says. "I have a gun." His speech is slightly slurred. He's been drinking, so he's probably going to behave irrationally. Just like Bruno did when he had too much lager in the afternoon.

I glance at the detective inspector and he catches hold of my arm as though he doesn't want me to leave him, even though my instincts are screaming at me to run and run and run. Shouting for help of course at the same time. If only I had my phone.

We were taught how to handle someone with a knife, but the recommendation was that unless we're just about to be shot, it's better to try to pacify a gunman and wait for them to make a mistake. The mistake I've made is coming here with DI Dickinson.

"The boss wants the book from your office, Mrs Jones," the man says.

"Book?" That's my first reaction. "What book? If you're looking for a notebook, Sam didn't leave one." I say Sam, because I can't think of any other reason for what's happening.

"Do as he says," the detective inspector says. He seems to be no help at all. Even so, I can't really believe he's in on this. He was with me in the office. He could have asked to borrow whatever book this man wants.

"*The Police Driver's Handbook*," the man says.

It's probably the tension, but I can't help laughing. Almost hysterically. "*That* book! There's nothing valuable about that, I can assure you. I've looked through it a couple of times as part of my training. There's nothing written in there, and not even a loose sheet of paper for a bookmark. I nearly didn't bring it with me when I moved here."

"Good thing you did," the man says. "I know we're rather late, but it's taken a long time to crack the encryption on your husband's phone. Now we've done that, we've seen a note about there being something special in that book. Now, just walk slowly, the pair of you, and we're going back to your office, Mrs Jones, and I'm going to collect the book. And you, Detective Inspector Dickinson, well, the boss says I have to deal with both of you. It's just a job to me."

This certainly didn't come in my training. I take a quick look backwards. The man has a folded newspaper over his arm, which is presumably concealing a handgun.

"We tried to get in," the man says. His speech is slurred. He's definitely drunk.

We? How many are there involved in Sam's death?

"Your locks are too good, and we know you have an alarm you set in the daytime when you're out." The man stops for a moment and gives a loud belch. "I could kill you both here and take the keys, but you'd probably give me the wrong code to the alarm before I shot you."

"You're welcome to the book," I say, trying to sound calm. "There's no need to kill us. We don't even know who you are." As if that's going to make a difference.

"The office," the man says. "And you, Detective Inspector Dickinson, get your phone out of your pocket and throw it over to me. Slowly. *Do it!*"

Roger Dickinson does as he's told. The man might be drunk, but his reflexes are still good enough to catch the phone with his free hand. He pushes it into his pocket. I can only hope this is not some elaborate trick the DI has dreamed up. Perhaps he has two phones, and is doing this to make me think he's on my side.

As we get towards Button Up, I'm desperately hoping Pete Wilders will be standing in the coffee shop window and realise something suspicious is going on. He likes playing detectives, so he told me, and he might phone the police, but probably too late. This man is going to grab the book, kill us, and disappear before the police can make an appearance. I'm guessing the gun has a silencer, but I haven't been able to see it.

Of course, there's no sign of Pete when we reach Button Up. As I get the door keys out of my bag, I'm holding the Sherlock Holmes key ring that Liam gave me. The kid is going to be devastated if anything happens to me. Well,

I hope *everyone* is going to be devastated, including my parents. Unfortunately, the figure of Sherlock Holmes is plastic and not a weapon in any shape or form. And the keys are too short to try to stab the gunman.

I take my time opening both locks on the outside door, but still no one comes.

"Unset the alarm, Mrs Jones," the man says. "No tricks. We wouldn't be here now if you hadn't made this place so secure. We had plans to come in one night and give you a surprise."

"I'm glad about that," I mutter under my breath. But he's obviously heard me.

"Different story, same ending. It's going to look as though you shot the Inspector and then killed yourself, because you blame the police for your husband's death. These things happen. Go on, up the stairs. Both of you." The door closes automatically behind us as we start slowly up the stairs and I hear the latch click firmly into place.

Without the key, the man isn't going to be able to escape after he's killed us. Abi is certainly in for a shock tomorrow when she comes round with her own key to see why I haven't come into Button Up for my cappuccino and croissant!

"And no talking – or I shoot you here."

I believe him. The man sounds drunk enough to do something crazy like that.

Roger Dickinson leads the way. I get the feeling he's about to tell me something, but he stays silent. The gunman's breath smells like Bruno's. I'm hoping he's unsteady on his feet. We're nearly at the top, when I pretend to stumble. The man comes closer. Much closer. His breath stinks so strongly of alcohol that I cough.

He prods me in the back with his gun, and it hurts. "Keep moving."

I raise my right foot as though I'm about to take the next step, but instead I kick back as hard as I can. The man is completely taken by surprise, and I hear him stumble backwards, but not before he manages to fire off a shot. It's not loud. The gun probably has a silencer.

I don't think I've been hit, and even if Roger Dickinson has, we're so nearly at the top that I can help him through the door.

I can see a splash of blood on the floor. I don't think it's mine.

I quickly unlock the door and shove the detective inspector into my office so hard that he falls over, but I'm not bothered. I slam the door shut and fix the metal bar in place, making us secure for the moment.

Roger Dickinson seems to be in a daze, holding his arm as though in pain. He must have been hit. I was expecting him to take charge, but no matter. My phone is where I left it on my desk at the detective inspector's instructions. I pick it up.

The man is pounding on the door, and throwing his weight against it. So far, the bar is holding. Roger Dickinson has suddenly come to life, and he grabs my phone from my hands, and dials. It's not the usual 999, because he gets straight through to some special emergency number.

The man is still throwing himself against the door. I hadn't intended it to stand up to this sort of treatment when I ordered it.

"Armed police are on their way," Roger says. "We'd better go through into your living room, in case he starts shooting through the door panel."

"We can do better than that," I say. "I've got an emergency escape through the back window. I take it you can climb down a rope ladder." I point to his arm. "Do you think you can manage?"

Roger puts his arm round me. I think it's the one that's bleeding, but I don't mind. It's good to be held at a time like this. "Just a flesh wound."

Roger is right about the gunman. He takes a couple of shots through the door, and then we hear him run down the stairs. Hopefully, the automatic lock at the bottom of the stairs will prevent his escape. There's a panic button in my bedroom, as well as under my desk. I never expected to need it in circumstances like this. I know help is on the way, but I press the button by my bed as Roger opens the window.

The DI is sharp. He sees where to hook the end of the coiled ladder onto the secure fitting below the windowsill inside the room, and throws the rest of it out. Meanwhile, the alarm is sounding loudly both inside and outside the building, and even more loudly on the staircase where it's designed to be loud enough to drive someone out of their mind.

Roger seems to be debating whether he or I should go first. Another shot comes from the staircase, penetrating the door. I don't care if it's damaged my lovely desk. At least he's not able to hit one of us.

Roger tries to lift me over the low windowsill, but I can see he's in pain now. I can manage by myself. Within seconds I'm on the ground, and I feel the ladder above me trembling as Roger Dickinson already has his feet on it. I really hope he can manage to hold on, in spite of his arm injury.

Above the noise of the alarm, I can hear emergency vehicles arriving. Within seconds, armed police are at the front and back of Button Up, and the team at the front are shouting to everyone to stay inside the café.

I go to grab my phone from Roger to warn Abi and everyone to get out of sight, but he's using it to convey instructions. I suppose in a film this would be exciting, but I'm scared stiff. *Absolutely* scared stiff.

It's nearly half an hour before we're allowed into the coffee shop to recover. It seems that Abi, realising that the police needed to get into my apartment, hurried out and offered them my spare keys.

The man has now gone, tasered and handcuffed, but the press are still hanging around. I need to speak to them. We were told on our course not to miss the opportunity for self advertising. Although I'm not going to take any credit for the capture, I want to put in a personal appearance, and hopefully get booked for a full interview and photo shoot at a later date. The sooner the better.

Roger Dickinson seems to have taken charge, and he assures the reporters and a television crew that a statement will be released shortly. He's already been examined by the medics and refused to go to the hospital, in spite of their insistence. So for the moment his arm is bandaged. It seems the bone didn't get hit.

I stand proudly as one of the photographers takes a low-level picture with me and my sign in the office window above. I don't want to attract clients who are on the business end of a gun, but it does make me feel professional. I've been told that the Button Up Detective Agency will shortly be on national television. How good is that!

I doubt my parents will be able to see any news about this in Poland. And how good is *that*!

Epilogue

It's gone six o'clock now, and although Abi has officially closed the coffee shop and locked up, Pete has pulled several tables together so that the whole group of us can sit down.

Roger Dickinson has gone. No doubt he's busy questioning the gunman. There's Abi and Danny here, Abi's friends Rupert and Alice Forrester who I've not really met yet, Melanie and Steve Donovan with young Liam, and Pete – with Hayley sitting on his lap even though there are plenty of empty chairs.

Outside, I can see people slowing down to have a good look through the large windows as they walk past, but the police and the press have gone, and there's nothing to see. Judging by the interest from the passers-by, I think Abi would do a roaring trade if she opened up for business.

There are three bullet holes in the door at the top of the stairs, and I'm wondering whether to leave them to impress clients. Perhaps it will scare the wrong people off. If Victor Armitage comes storming up the stairs to complain about my interference in his love life, I'll just nod and smile, and point to the three holes. And I gather Liam Donovan is already demanding to see them!

Mrs Miller contacted me a few minutes ago to tell me

how successful my plan had been with her daughter and Mr Armitage. She had contacted Mrs Cooke and asked her to leave the back gate open for her and Laura, and at five o'clock on the dot the brazen hussy had arrived in all her finery, to quote Mrs Miller.

I gather there had been such a scene in the road that most of the residents had come out to witness the fight. Do I feel sorry for Laura? Not a bit of it. I wish I'd had a mother like that, instead of one who more or less forced me into a relationship with Bruno.

As soon as the apartment was declared safe, Roger Dickinson and I made straight for my small collection of books. *The Police Driver's Handbook* was among them. I had once studied it in case there was some useful advice about high-speed chases, but I would have been wasting my time with my little Nissan Micra. And I still haven't taken it to Rupert Forrester for him to sort out.

Then it came to me. I remembered how Sam had seemed obsessed with that book in the days before he was killed. I pulled his leg about it, saying there was some hope of us chasing anyone in our Micra. He said he wanted to jot down a few things while he remembered them.

Roger Dickinson and I checked the book page by page from front to back, and couldn't find anything handwritten. It's a paperback so there was nothing hidden in the spine. What had Sam wanted to jot down, and where had he done it? I couldn't remember seeing a pad of paper with him. Just a silver ballpoint pen.

Of course! I remembered the game Sam and I played

at Christmas with our secret messages written with UV ink with our special silver pens. In my kit I keep a bright ultraviolet lamp. I grabbed it and switched it on. Written inside the back cover we found several names, in Sam's handwriting. Roger Dickinson said he felt frustrated that they had missed it on the search of the house immediately following Sam's death, but I told him they were hardly expected to check every single book for invisible ink.

Roger Dickinson has taken the book as evidence. Although for security reasons I wasn't allowed to examine the names closely, apparently Sam had written possible suspects in the gang of drug dealers. Why there? Perhaps he wasn't confident enough about the names to pass them on, but had jotted them down using the UV pen so I would be unlikely to read them and get involved. And the book was handy at the time. Had he gone that fatal night to follow up one of these names, to meet someone he trusted?

Someone with more brains than the gunman must have worked out how to access Sam's phone – eventually. But if they had got hold of the book, would they have had enough brains to search for the UV ink?

I almost feel sorry for Detective Inspector Roger Dickinson, having to send his wife and children into hiding. He seems uncertain as to when it will be safe for them to come back. The gunman on the stairs was, to use the DI's earlier description, no more than one of the branches. Hopefully, he will lead the police to the root, and the tree of evil will die. So at the moment I may not be completely safe.

Perhaps Sam has left more information behind. I'm going to search every single page of every single book in my apartment with my UV light.

I'm fingering Sam's gold cross, still on its thin leather cord. It meant a lot to Sam, but I'm not ready to wear it – not yet. Maybe never. I don't want to be a fraud. Abi's just invited me to her church on Sunday morning. I can't really believe there's something there for me. I prayed a few times when Bruno was at his worst, when I lost the baby. Anybody would pray in those circumstances. Did God hear? Abi and some of the others seem to have found something I'm looking for.

Liam has been listening, and he comes over and whispers that I can sit near the front with him and his friends, Sophie and William. He says everyone may sing what he calls his "best ever church song." As far as I can gather, it's about a sheep lost in a storm in the snow on a dark mountain.

Apparently the shepherd in the song looked for it because he loved it, even though it had deliberately run away. Maybe I need that sort of love and acceptance. No, perhaps I need *that* love! What would Sam say?

THE END

The Abi Button Book Series

Tall Men and Strangers is the first Abi Button Cozy Mystery Romance.

Abigail (Abi) Button is thirty-one, and in spite of kissing a few frogs she has yet to find her prince. On the lookout for a tall, dark stranger (but not too strange) she realises he has been living locally all the time. It's just that she has not really noticed Jack Thornley until she meets him in her road late one evening, standing by an emergency ambulance.

Abi's elderly neighbour is Ivy Smith, and she's ninety-one. She gives Abi a small silver key, telling her to keep it secret from her nephew Jack who is helping to care for her. What the key opens, Abi has no idea.

Ivy worries that she hears someone moving around her house at night, when she should be alone. Abi tries to reassure her by saying it's only the old house settling at night, or noisy neighbours, but Ivy Smith is unconvinced. Soon Abi is unconvinced, too.

As Abi's friendship with Jack develops, he invites her to his local church where she meets Danny Wells. Much to her embarrassment she remembers kissing Danny at school. Old memories start to surface, threatening to put the relationship with Jack in jeopardy.

A cozy mystery romance taking place in a small English town, told by Abi Button.

Poetry and Mayhem is the second Abi Button Cozy Mystery Romance.

Abi Button gets involved with the lazy nephews and nieces of their elderly uncle who lived in the creepy house at the far end of her road. Isaac Whittard Magritte Newton, to give him his full name, has set a cryptic clue in his will for the siblings to solve. The will says the first nephew or niece who can solve the clue is going to be extremely wealthy, but the puzzle seems unbreakable. The old man once set crossword puzzles for two of the national newspapers, and other puzzles for various magazines. Abi, with her modest skills in cryptic crosswords, has to admit defeat.

Also on Abi's mind, perhaps as a matter of greater importance than solving the clue that will help four squabbling siblings, is her developing friendship with junior solicitor Danny Wells. She wonders if she has at last found the right man. Melanie Upton – Abi's co-owner of Button Up coffee shop – assures Abi that this one is definitely a keeper. But as Abi points out, Melanie says the same thing about every man Abi gets to know.

Cake and Calamity, the third Abi Button Cozy Mystery Romance.

"Organising a wedding is a piece of cake," to quote Abigail (Abi) Button. She could be right, because a local wedding shop provides the whole service: bridal gowns, venue, cake, food, cars ... everything that makes the perfect wedding. Apart from husbands!

Meanwhile, Melanie Upton – Abi Button's co-owner of Button Up coffee shop – confides in Abi that romance is in the air with an Italian property investor called Romero Rocco. Can it be true?

Abi's new friend and neighbour is also getting married. She now owns the house Abi calls Creepy Mansion. She says getting a builder to restore the old house should also be a simple matter. So with a joint wedding planned for Abi and her new friend, Abi asks, "What can possibly go wrong?"

A cozy mystery romance taking place in the small English town of Craidlea, told by Abi Button.

Ghouls and Jewels, the fourth Abi Button Cozy Mystery Romance.

Abi returns from her honeymoon to find a threatening letter on the doormat. Her new friend Alice says her sister and brothers are claiming she's secretly in possession of a priceless Russian tiara and associated jewels, and they insist on having their share – and they are already arranging to take her to court.

This is news to Alice, so Abi and Alice, with their new husbands set out to search the creepy old house that Alice has recently purchased.

A neighbour says she has heard wailing coming from the house, and Abi's childhood fear that the house is haunted seems to be confirmed when she sees a woman's face staring out between the bars of a basement window at night.

The search for the Russian treasure leads to an unpleasant encounter with a dominating father and aunt. More problems for Abi to solve, in between running Button Up coffee shop with her co-owner Melanie Upton, who has romantic news to share. This time it sounds as though it could be promising – with just one small drawback.

Doughnuts and Disaster, the fifth Abi Button Cozy Mystery Romance.

It's late February and the area is experiencing an unexpected cold snap with snow. Liam, Steve Donovan's eight-year-old son, is staying with Abi while Steve and Melanie are on their honeymoon.

Abi is concerned when single mum Bethany reports a man wearing a long raincoat, hanging around the local play area taking photographs. Bethany is afraid that her father and disagreeable Aunt Erica have sent him to spy on her, with a view to snatching baby Freddie. Abi thinks there are two men watching. Why two?

Young Liam is clearly upset by all the changes in his life, and Abi tries to win his confidence with jam donuts. Abi warns Liam and his friends to keep away from the deep pond in the woods, because the ice is too thin to walk on. But Liam is on the hunt for Bigfoot, convinced he lives somewhere amongst the trees.

Bethany's friendship with Harry the builder seems to be turning into a romance, maybe even a wedding – if Bethany's father and Aunt Erica can be kept away. Pete and Hayley also wonder if this is a good opportunity to discuss marriage!

A cozy mystery romance taking place in the small English town of Craidlea, told by Abi Button.

Apple Pie and Follies, the sixth and final Abi Button Cozy Mystery Romance.

Alice and Rupert Forrester have just moved into the house Abi used to call Creepy Castle. The basement apartment will soon be ready for newlywed Bethany and Harry with baby Freddie. Alice finds an old map of the area in the college library, which leads to some exciting discoveries.

Some items donated to the local cat charity cause serious problems for Abi and Danny, with Danny locked in a police cell and suspended from work at lawyers Branks, Davis & Waters, and Abi taken in for questioning. Meanwhile, life at Button Up coffee shop proceeds in the usual way – a way that is often far from normal.

Button Up Detective Agency
The Button Up Spin-off Series

Clocks Locks and Danger

A Button Up Detective Agency Cozy Mystery #1

This book.

Hugs Bugs and Danger

A Button Up Detective Agency Cozy Mystery #2

As Janika Jones settles into her new career as a private investigator – fully trained, of course – she is asked to take the part of a New York art collector's assistant to investigate a picture in a London art gallery, where she has to obtain vital photographic evidence without being caught. The theft of a collection of wartime medals leads to a gruesome discovery. And being accused of poisoning an unwelcome visitor is just another event in Janika's hectic life at the Button Up Detective Agency.

Shoes Clues and Danger

A Button Up Detective Agency Cozy Mystery #3

When Janika Jones started the Button Up Detective Agency, she was reluctant to get involved in matrimonial problems. However, a desperate call from a woman whose life could be in danger convinces Janika that she needs to take action, urgently.

Meanwhile, Piers Pillinger wants Janika to carry out another job involving Humphrey Broxburn, the owner of a West End art gallery. Piers assures Janika that she is in no danger and she can trust Humphrey absolutely, but when she is bundled into a blacked out vehicle in the centre of London, she wonders who has been deceiving who.

A major theft from the Mill Lane Garage where Rupert Forrester works makes suspicion fall on Rupert who was last to leave and should have locked up and set the alarm. But did he forget? Janika gets assistance from Toby Walton as she tries to track down the thief and put Rupert in the clear. As Janika says about Toby, "He's not really my boyfriend." But Abi and Alice have other ideas.

Told by Janika Jones, this is the third slightly darker spin-off from the series of six *Abi Button Cozy Mystery Romance* books, also by Lizzie Lewis. Although mainly about Janika, she interacts with many of the main Abi Button story characters.

Kicks Tricks and Danger

A Button Up Detective Agency Cozy Mystery #4

Janika Jones' early morning jog round the park, and her interview on local TV, lead to unexpected danger. Meanwhile, her relationship with Toby Walton proceeds well, until he shares more of his past life. Janika is concerned there may be a side to Toby that she hadn't suspected, and she starts to feel uneasy. An elderly lady is being targeted by a conman, and Janika perhaps unwisely tells the lady to hand over the money as evidence of a crime.

Young Liam Donovan goes with Janika on a stakeout as mother and son, with Janika wearing a ginger wig to avoid suspicion. She assures Melanie the boy will be completely safe. But at the crucial moment, Liam decides he's going to be a hero. And of course the celebratory meal at Parke's with Janika and Courtney Jacobs doesn't go at all as planned. This is the fourth *Button Up Detective Agency* book featuring Janika Jones, and some characters from the *Abi Button Cozy Mystery* series of six books.

Cards Shards and Danger

A Button Up Detective Agency Cozy Mystery #5

A second attempt to hold the previously abandoned celebratory meal at Parke's with Janika, Toby, Courtney and Ollie ends once again in catastrophe. There are accusations all round, but who is innocent and who is being set up? Janika wants to help sort out the innocent from the guilty, because she's about to be arrested for a crime she didn't commit. And Courtney is suspended from the CID.

Amabelia Flores, who is opening a small flower shop just up the road from Button Up, is suspected of giving false evidence about Janika to the police. But why would she do that? What harm has Janika done to her? And when Janika looks into the florist's background, she discovers a suspicious past – or is there something important that she has yet to discover?

Janika and Courtney hold their own investigation into the accusations which are the subject of two separate police enquiries, and try to find the connection. Toby Walton? Fortunately for Janika, he's still hanging in there – for now. Then their investigation takes them all to the edge of disaster.

Phones Bones and Danger

A Button Up Detective Agency Cozy Mystery #6

Coming spring 2022

When Daisy Evans, a.k.a. Amabelia (Bella) Flores gets the result of a DNA test she has done in an attempt to discover her unknown father, things don't work out well, and she risks losing her new florist business. Bella asks Janika Jones to investigate, and the result is something neither of them expected.

Janika is also investigating aliens who are apparently landing at night in the field behind Nigel Frampton's house. Unsurprisingly, the police show no interest at all, so Nigel hires Janika to set up a surveillance camera. Janika has to hope no one finds out what she's doing, or she will become a laughing stock. However, it turns out that the job is far from laughable, and there's serious danger involved.

Piers Pillinger wants to make use of Janika's photographic skills again, and assures her this is a perfectly straightforward job at his own home. Nothing can possibly go wrong – and Janika believes him!

Toby Walton? Well....